In a Company of Fiddlers

In a Company
of Fiddlers

by
Rob Ritchie

Seraphim
EDITIONS

The publisher gratefully acknowledges the financial assistance of the Canada Council for the Arts.

 Canada Council **Conseil des Arts**
for the Arts **du Canada**

Library and Archives Canada Cataloguing in Publication

Ritchie, Rob, 1964-
    In a company of fiddlers / by Rob Ritchie.

ISBN 978-1-927079-00-3

    I. Title.

PS8635.I82I5 2011   C813'.6   C2011-905394-2

Editor: George Down
Author Photo: Robi Walters
Cover Design and Typography: Julie McNeill, McNeill Design Arts

Published in 2011 by
Seraphim Editions
54 Bay Street
Woodstock, ON
Canada N4S 3K9

Printed and bound in Canada

For Betty Ritchie

*… and for all of her friends who gather around
the MacNay kitchen table to discuss music.
And in loving memory of Ken, who poured the tea.*

Special Thanks to:

Maureen Whyte for sticking with me, George Down for his tireless efforts in forming this tale into a novel, Trudi Down for all the wonderful promotion, and McNeill Design Arts for their sharp creative eye.

A heart-felt thanks also to those whose friendship has played a role in weaving together this story. This begins with each and every person who has taught me to love and appreciate music. I am truly indebted. Thanks also to Charlie Grube and Tim Sosinski for their insights on the joys and influence of architecture, to Steve Ritchie for his expertise on acoustics, and to Ande Ritchie for ever deepening my understanding of adoption. As well, I would like to thank all the brave souls whom I had the privilege of talking with during an 18-month stint as a Distress Centre volunteer many years ago.

Finally, thank you to my family, Ande, Josh and Toby for all of their love and support.

Prologue

The snow is a bright new blanket across the distant fields, its cover reflecting the light of the full December moon back into the frosted air. He glances back at the farmhouse. Two blue spotlights shine up from the ground bathing the rough sandy-coloured stone in a warm glow. It's not the busy multi-light display that is the order of the season for so many houses, but – as he could have predicted – a most accurate measure of mood and shading. Visual phrasing. Dynamics of the eye.

The dog runs on ahead. Though the farm is her home she will not stay close tonight, busy as she is with her tasks of sniffing, pawing and running; with instincts which, even after a life of domesticity, all too easily outdistance the duties of a loyal pet. He tries to call for her, to keep her close for his own comfort's sake. And though at times he thinks she briefly cocks her ear in recognition, her enthusiasm for the night prevails and, just as quickly, she is back at full speed, bounding up the lane.

He turns to follow but hesitates at the sight of the barn in front of him and for a moment is lost in its dereliction. Now but a shadow of its history; a skeleton of wooden beam and crumbling stone, it was once home to livestock and machinery, ventilated for summer with well-measured barnboard; heated in winter with the steamy breath of dozens of cattle residing within, it had been almost organic the way it had lived, and – he notes yet again – the way it had died, slowly receding into the very ground where it had for generations been so rooted. Now only the silo remains, paradoxically straight and strong, its smooth stone walls still reaching for the sky.

His thoughts turn to the concert hall so far away. They will be seated by now, he reasons. Positioned adequately, he hopes, to feel the soloists' presence but still far enough removed to receive the full blend of the choral work. That would be his preference, at least.

His spell is broken by the dog's impatient bark as she claws away at some loose stones along the barnyard's fenceline. He looks back once more, then turns away from the light.

Sinfony

EMERSON PLACE PRESENTS

MESSIAH
An oratorio in three parts

by
George Frideric Handel
(1685-1759)

The Toronto Chorus and the Metropolitan Symphony
Walter Engels conducting
Sarah Ibramovich, concert mistress

Margaret Calloway *soprano*
Gloria Devereaux *alto*
Neil Raynsford *tenor*
Trevor Messon *bass*

The unseasonably warm weather had mobilized the city that afternoon. Eating and drinking establishments had hastily dusted off their outdoor furniture, unwound their awnings and umbrellas, swept up and hosed down their patios of any remaining sludge still clinging from winter's grip, quickly readying themselves for the onslaught of workforce that would soon emerge from office and tower dragging behind it the suddenly unnecessary weight of trench coats and parkas as its members doffed ties and loosened scarves, so ripe for the option of a drink or a meal in the unexpected sun. Once out, the liberated masses would join the joggers and bikers, the power walkers and stroller-pushers, already heeding climate's call, scurrying from their skin-bleached hibernation in shorts and sneakers as they crowded the parks and sidewalks and footpaths with flushed faces and heavy breath. By late afternoon playgrounds would be teeming with the giddy, pent-up energy of toddlers and preschoolers for whom the long winter had represented so great a portion of their young lives. Young and old, rich and poor, from the penthouses and condos right down to the underbelly of the city. Yes, the downtrodden too – the begging and the homeless – had returned to take up their warm-weather positions from balmy days past. Returned to their street corners, their fences, their park benches, to their preferred locations only snow and frostbite had ever bid them reluctantly abandon. Back from the warmer, safer confines of hostels and shelters. Back home.

Perhaps this would be his starting point, Peter decided, as he sat patiently at his favourite table of his favourite bistro; a discussion of the existing social conditions of 18th-century Ireland – the backdrop prevalent at the time in the country where Handel's *Messiah* had first been performed. How the resident poor had been displaced from their land by English landlords, persecuted for a Catholic faith by an insistent and intolerant brand of Anglicanism so championed by that usurping class. How, once disenfranchised, they had roamed aimlessly, eventually migrating to the cities – the largest, of course, being Dublin – where they soon formed an impoverished stratum of significant size. And indeed, hadn't a good number of the early performances of *Messiah* only been allowed by Church powers on the proviso they be sanctioned as fundraisers for the religious charities that tended to these poor classes? And didn't it seem the pertinent introduction, given the fact Peter himself had almost stepped on a homeless man sprawled in a heap across the sidewalk, just as he was stepping into the patio to get to his seat? Moreover, since Kyle was meeting him directly from his seminar class, there was little doubt some hotly-debated theory about social work would still be dominating his thoughts anyway.

For him to relax – truly relax and appreciate the concert the way Peter hoped he would – the way Peter himself always did – he would need to be eased into the evening slowly. Last month's attempt at opera over at the O'Keefe had taught the young music major as much. Poor Kyle, rushing in from a fruitless day in the university library, grumpy, nothing to eat, and suddenly plopped down beside that uptight couple for a whole night of *Rigoletto*, when the poor man had never so much as been to a classical concert before in his life. The good news, with which Peter now consoled himself once again, was that the whole fiasco had proved just how much Kyle cared for him, phoning the next day to apologize, asking him not to give up on a bitchy social scientist's musical education; asking for patience. "Baby steps to culture," as Kyle had put it.

And so they agreed to try again, this time with the promise of a few pints of Guinness, a nice meal at a safe and comfortable establishment, and lots of time to sit and chat so Peter could offer some background and history to the music they were about to take in. And what better primer to the world of choral music than Handel's grandest oratorio?

He glanced over at the hunched shoulders, the weathered cheeks of the man he had almost tripped on and wondered for a moment whether his beloved Handel might have been forced to step over some similar-looking figure, on his way into Fishamble Musick Hall, back in 1741. He watched as the man fumbled with a roll of quarters, aligning them, counting them, wrapping them, returning them so carefully to the tired grimy folds of his overcoat. Taking them out again. Counting them once more. He wondered how many others had walked by the man. How many more people than the coins he now lovingly tallied had stared straight ahead, increasing their foot speed when they heard his plea for spare change, averting their eyes as they busied themselves with some phantom immediate concerns in their pockets or purses? How many had even considered stopping, to toss a quarter down, even say hello or ask how he was doing? "Strange the polarized reaction of a passing city on her homeless," Peter recalled Kyle's insightful words from back on their very first date two months ago. "The unconcerned write them off as a menace to society. The romantic presents them as misunderstood poets and geniuses. Truth is they float around somewhere in the middle. And to insist on placing them in one camp or the other, well it's really just asking them to perform, isn't it?"

This was why he loved Kyle, he decided. Kyle was in the middle of this spectrum and yet in no way weighed down by either end. He was at once the idealist who refused to be hardened by the scale of his city's social ills, and the generous and tireless activist who would never sacrifice an individual's suffering for some abstract theory of the greater good. "Every person is deserving of telling his or her story," he had said back on that first night out, and indeed Peter had heard the mantra from his boyfriend's lips many times since, listening as he debated and defended his particular motivations to friends and peers, in coffee shops and at house parties. Everyone is deserving of telling his or her story. If it could be true, Peter mused freely now, then his beloved Kyle – grad student by day, shelter worker and social agency volunteer by night-after-night – he, by his very resolve – was these stories' means. Their voice. Their audience. Their concert.

~DECEMBER 11, 2010~

Allison Page glanced to the seat next to her and let out a long low breath of satisfaction. She had done it. She had successfully urged, guided and manoeuvred the legendary Margaret Calloway back to the concert hall that she had herself christened twenty-eight years before. And while the implementation of her plan had proved far more strenuous than the fleeting notion that had first inspired it – all the way from home, down the length of Highway 10 and into the middle of Toronto, then parking, then arranging some dinner – the sense of accomplishment certainly warranted a moment's reward.

Allison marvelled at the sight of her. She was now somewhere in her late seventies – Maggie had never found the need to divulge the specifics of her age – and though now shrunken with the illnesses of age and dwarfed by the plush upholstery of her chair, Allison still found a presence there.

Still saw a dancing in the eyes, still felt the passion of her most musical soul. They were the very qualities that had enchanted the young woman since she was a child. Qualities she herself had aspired to. Or at the very least, as some liked to remind her, had aspired to be near. Maggie appeared alert, which was a good thing. Better still, her body seemed reasonably comfortable, any shakiness or weariness that the three-hours-plus car ride might have wrought having subsided with the woman's anticipation of the first bow strokes of the grand work which had, above all other performances, so defined her professional career.

Allison had picked Maggie up at nine-thirty that morning, her minivan outfitted meticulously for transporting the woman's frailty. There were blankets for the cold, a warm thermos of tea ready in the cupholder, pillows and cushions for stuffing beneath and around any part of the body that might require gentle bolstering. There was the sectioned tray laid ready with her daily medications to be administered throughout the trip as outlined by Rita, the live-in nurse, who had, at the eleventh hour, reluctantly agreed to the preposterous idea that had sponsored their day. And of course there was the boxed set of CDs, Handel's *Messiah*, at the ready for the car stereo, should Maggie wish to hear some selections as a teaser for the night ahead. It was their favourite version, the Philips 250th anniversary recording. The one they had enjoyed for the past ten years, ever since Allison had returned home to take the position of music teacher at the local secondary school and had assumed the directorship of the local community choir, infusing it with repertoire beyond the English shanties and barbershop harmonies that had greeted her upon her arrival. And indeed the CDs proved a good idea. The two had listened through most of the oratorio, Allison singing along to the alto chorus lines comfortably from memory, and Maggie, for her part, mouthing breathily her favourite passages from the soprano's solos, occasionally waving a bony arm and calling out hoarse instruction, as if the recording were subject to her directions. "Not too fast," she would mutter time and again, almost like a plea, as she gently but repeatedly pushed the air in front of her with the palms of her hands, just as she always did whenever the two of them got together to listen to music. Over the last several years those occasions became institutionalized into a Saturday afternoon tradition, with Allison driving out to Maggie's home, putting on the tea and getting her friend lounging comfortably on the sofa in her parlour, sometimes for a radio broadcast from the Met in New York, sometimes a selection of Maggie's choosing from the Calloway record library in the lower hallway. And just like it did on almost every one of those occasions, the music inevitably overtook the woman as she rode along down the highway, leaning back in the car seat, her eyes closed in a blend of concentration and bliss, her hands moving to caress the music out of the air. "Yes ... yes, not too fast ... not too fast ..." Maggie Calloway did not like her music rushed.

Allison glanced over one more time, just as the concert mistress entered and raised her bow to signal the orchestra's preparation, nodding for an oboe to supply the long lean note by which all the other instruments would perfect their pitch. Maggie's elbows had found the armrests of her chair. Her fingers were folded together and cradled her chin. Her expression was equal parts aged and childlike; proof positive that the evening was indeed a success. All the impediments to their adventure, all the many mitigating forces that had at first conspired to curtail Allison's optimism could now safely recede. The day was unalterable. The sense of doing something profoundly meaningful was all that remained. She had brought the great Margaret Calloway back to see the concert stage that Allison's mentor had once graced herself ... with nothing more to await but the genius of George Frideric Handel, about to unfold before them.

●

Hello. You've reached the Toronto Distress Line. This is Corrine speaking.

    – Is Andrew there?

No … I'm Corinne. But if you'd like to talk I'd be glad to-

    – I want Andrew. Andrew 03.

Is this Eli? … hello …?

    – Is he there?

Eli. You know the rules. We can't divulge who works at the call centre and we can't fulfill requests to speak with specific people. However, if you wish I can have a conversation with you for a few minutes.

    – Fifteen minutes. I get fifteen minutes. They said last night.

Did you phone us last night, Eli?

    – But the bastard hung up after eleven.

I'm sure they didn't mean to-

    – I have a clock right here.

Well I promise not to cut you off early, Eli.

    – Fifteen minutes?

Fifteen minutes. No more, no less.

    – Unless I was in real trouble, correct? If there was some sort of danger?

And are you in danger, Eli? … Hello …?

    – Fifteen minutes. Promise me.

I already did promise, Eli.

    – I have a clock right in front of me.

Yes, you mentioned that. So, what would you like to talk about tonight?

    – I was downtown this afternoon. Where they're going to build the new concert hall.

You mean Emerson Place?

    – Yes I do.

And how does it look? Have they started construction yet?

— *Its design will be for large symphonic and choral works with a focus on acoustics and sightlines.*

I suppose it will.

— *... with an opening scheduled for April of 1982. The first concert will be the annual performance of Handel's* Messiah *with The Metropolitan Symphony and The Toronto Chorus under the direction of Walter Engels.*

And do you like classical music, Eli?

— *Choral music.*

I'm sorry?

— *I'm talking about choral music, you idiot.*

Now Eli ...

— *Every ignorant jackass just jumps to the term classical music. Do I know anything about a concerto? No. Did I say anything about a symphonic work? No. I said Handel's Messiah. Which is an oratorio. And an oratorio by definition is choral music, you ignorant fool!*

Eli, I'm going to ask you to calm down or our fifteen-minute deal is off.

— *Do I like it, she asks. What kind of hopelessly innocuous question is that? Like I could just take or leave the whole thing! Like I have some sort of goddamn choice in the matter!*

ELI!

— *I know what you idiots do down there, you know. I know you have a file on me. I bet you're taking goddamn notes right now!*

Eli, if you can't compose yourself-

— *Goddamn files. Do I like it, she asks.*

This is your last warning.

— *Goddamn idiots.*

OK we're through here. I'm hanging up. Good-bye, Eli.

— What? No, please ... wait!

Not when you're being abusive like this.

— No. I'm sorry. Please don't hang up. It's so hard to get through. Please, it's so goddamn hard. I'm sorry ...

Can you compose yourself?

— No ... I mean, yes. Look, I just need to talk to somebody sometimes.

I know. And that's OK ... that's fine.

— There's just so much tension.

Well then, let's talk about that. Because you know what, Eli? When you aren't being abusive, you show a tremendous amount of courage. Just by recognizing your need to talk to someone. That's a very brave thing. Do you realize how brave you are, Eli?

-I'm just alone. That's all.

And loneliness is a terrible thing. So many people have a family member or a friend they can call. Maybe a clergyman or a work colleague. You're very strong for calling here, Eli. I want you to know that ... Eli ...?

— I saw the new hall today.

So you said, yes.

Its design will be for large symphonic and choral works with a focus on acoustics and sightlines ...

Yes, you mentioned that too.

●

The idea first struck Allison while visiting her grandfather for a cup of tea one Tuesday afternoon. Murray Page lived in Room 213 of the Assisted Independent Living Wing of Sunset Haven. It had been his home ever since the stroke he took back in the fall of 2004.

Sunset Haven as a whole was a quiet building set back from the street at the end of a gently curving laneway lined with hedges and raised flower beds that some of the more industrious residents tended themselves. Murray's room, however, faced the back lawn, a sprawling roll of greenery mowed meticulously by a groundskeeper with an equally close-cropped crewcut. This amused Murray mildly from time to time, as did much of the goings-on in the institution whenever he had a stroll about, which, truth be told, was not all that often – for, given his druthers, Murray Page preferred the company of his own room, a tidy little space that appealed to his sense of both solitude and order, accommodating all he still needed in life and absolutely nothing more. Like camping a bit, he had thought on his first night's stay, after finding neat and logical places for all of his personal effects.

There was a table opposite his bed that served as a desktop where he could spread out the evening paper or go to work on a jigsaw puzzle. There was a small TV bracketed to the wall which was turned on strictly to keep up with the news of the day. A small pine wardrobe … an adjustable twin-size bed and, perhaps most fortuitously, one long east-facing window whose vantage allowed the sun to spill into the room every morning, over the table, over his bedspread, and out across the perpetually buffed and polished floor. Light by which he could mark the day. Light that was still bright and natural; light that still borrowed from the world at large; light that greeted him there, after his very first sleep, and showed him that he could be content with this small and simple space.

Such was an important – even if undiscussed – consideration for both the man and his dwelling. For indeed he was, perhaps as everyone is, a product of the homes he had kept throughout his life. The rooms, the hallways, the closets, the space he had allotted for his own, be they back at the old house on Elm Street where his granddaughter now lived or in the private suite where he now abided; these details were not mere reflections of a homeowner's tastes, but indeed influences at work – their very size and contour ever defining their owner's character, ever honing Murray Page into the honest, neat and tidy, thrifty man that he was. Though the kind of man, it should also be noted, who would rarely entertain such speculation about himself. This despite the fact that ample time for self-reflection was also a prominent feature of Room 213 in the Assisted Independent Living Wing of Sunset Haven.

True, there had been the documentary he had watched on the Public Broadcast Station the week before. A biography of Churchill's career in politics and his philosophy on the world. Specifically the quote attributed to Sir Winston about architecture ... the one the narrator offered up just as the elderly viewer was starting to doze off. "*We shape our buildings ... thereafter they shape us.*" Perhaps that should have granted the man permission to reflect on his relationship with the spaces he called home. Churchill was, after all, something of a hero and all. But alas Murray Page did not see himself as a Churchill, so something like a *"just never liked a particularly big place"* would have most likely been his own extent on the subject, had he been pressed into an opinion. And in the end, perhaps it was this simplicity – this straightforwardness – that had, more than anything else, made the transition to the Haven a relatively seamless one. He still had his memories of a life with Helen. He still had a granddaughter close by. And while the stroke had taken away some facility with a bit of language recall, for the most part, thanks to therapy and to Allison's tending, he had bounced back quite nicely. He still had his truck. Still took it out for a drive so long as the weather was favourable. Over to the arena. Maybe out the shore road a ways. He was living comfortably day-to-day, seemingly in agreement with the march of time ... save for one small detail.

It was something that only rarely seeped into his thoughts, but nevertheless in a recurring fashion. And with its recurrence came somewhat of a snowball effect, sufficient in degree that on the Tuesday afternoon in question, with Allison already there at his door, it once again found its voice. "Let's have our tea up here today," Murray heard himself say, as he emptied his one and only chair of the neatly-piled magazines and newspapers that sat in wait for recycling pickup, then poured from a steeped pot that he had asked the kitchen to have sent up.

He began in the particularly slow and deliberate manner that Allison knew well was the signal that Grandpa had something weighing on his mind, beginning by stating that he was worried about her, though as soon as the thought was conveyed, and though the message was immediately tempered with a litany of self-effacing disclaimers on how he "*didn't mean to pry*" or "*stick a nose in where it don't belong*" because "*I'm the last guy who should be telling somebody else how to live their life*", it nevertheless managed to communicate the man's specific concern. He could not help wondering whether his granddaughter wasn't wasting her best years stuck back in her little home town "*hanging around with seniors*" … still single and without prospects for, "*you know … starting a family*" … too busy being a sidekick in other people's lives to move forward with her own. "*Whether that's your teaching, or your singing, or what-have-you.*"

She had heard him speak his mind on this before. Her initial response was to quickly shake her head and insist that helping look after the man who had single-handedly raised her was no burden whatsoever, but something in her grandfather's look on this particular Tuesday afternoon interrupted her gratitude.

"But you're not talking about yourself, are you, Grandpa?"

Grandpa stared straight ahead.

"You mean Maggie, don't you?" she said quietly.

"Well like I said, I'm no authority on life or anything. It's just when I think how fast things have gone by for me, and don't get me wrong, I wouldn't have traded the chance to raise you for anything. Anything at all. But if a person had dreams or aspirations of their own, Ally … and well, if those dreams were being held back because they were … well …"

"Were what, Grandpa?"

"Well maybe you're just a little bit too scared to break away … There, I said it."

"Too scared?"

"Look I'm sorry, but what about your own singing, Ally? Maggie herself used to say you could go places with a voice like yours. And if anyone would know-"

"That's all quite a while ago now, Grandpa."

"Not to me it isn't! Not at all. To me, it's all just sped right by. And now it seems like that old coot is more the problem than any help, the way she relies on you for all of her visits. Coming by each and every Saturday. Remember now, I'm the one who first got you lessons from that woman. I know how persuasive a sort she is …"

"Oh yeah? Is that from your little drinking dates way back when?" His granddaughter reached over and cuffed his knee, the needling smile on her face doing nothing to assure Murray he was being taken at all seriously.

"That's neither here nor there. Anyway, you're the one who's still all tied up in her dealings, Young Lady. Not me. I mean it's not as if she hasn't got any family of her own to look after her-"

"Oh Grandpa." Allison leaned over and gave him a dismissively fat kiss on his forehead that nevertheless let him know that she was, at least, unoffended by his concern. "Maggie's been so good to me. Good to us. And I like going out to her place. I look forward to it. It's not a duty. Just like coming here isn't."

Murray sighed. Deep down he knew this to be true. He had seen it himself on so many occasions, right from the time he had dropped her off for her very first singing lesson. Had seen it more clearly when he returned the hour later to find such unexpected spark in what had been such otherwise lifeless eyes. And when Allison had returned to town as an adult, rekindling their friendship at a time when it appeared Maggie had no other sources nor other desire for camaraderie, the spark had reignited. Murray saw it every time Ally shared with him some anecdote from a Saturday afternoon at the Calloway homestead ... perhaps some story about some performance Maggie gave years before in London or San Francisco ... perhaps a story prompted from a particular musical phrase or passage that the two would have been listening to. And though he often found himself lost in the details of her recollections, especially those concerning the finer points of choral music, or some pun based on musical notation, or some gossip about a famous musician that Maggie once crossed paths with, he nevertheless still sat and listened to all of it, because even now, twenty years later, whenever his granddaughter embarked on these stories, she was still completely alight.

Perhaps that was what troubled him about the relationship. That the dependency he perceived was not Maggie's alone. But he couldn't be sure. All he knew for certain was that whenever the inkling began to gnaw at him – as it had on that particular Tuesday afternoon – it was the one and only time the old man felt cramped in his surroundings. Not for himself, but for her. Because the truth was Allison Page still lived in the house where she was raised; a house she had seemingly hastened through university to return to; a house that she should have passed by long ago. And while it had sufficed for her childhood years, more and more he found himself worrying about its limitations. What if she wanted to settle down someday? Meet somebody? Maybe have some kids? With a kitchen that small? And those two tiny bedrooms? It was barely 900 square feet front to back. A 'starter home' as Murray had noted the paper's real estate section now called them. It made the old man restless. Made him pace his polished floor. Made him wish for more stops along the way for his beloved granddaughter. More stops before she – one day all too soon – also found herself stuffed into a tiny little room in an Assisted Independent facility.

"Besides," Allison broke off a second kiss, this time with her arms en-circling her grandfather's faded hairline. "Maggie's been failing quite a bit lately. I want to cherish the time I have with her while I can. Down the road, if I get feeling like I need to change paths-"

"Down the road sneaks up awful fast, Young Lady. That's all I'm saying."

And there they were, the succinct words of wisdom that would become the seeds of her idea when she revisited the conversation later that night. And although that idea would not fully germinate until four o'clock the next morning, and although it could be argued the idea actually – in one sense – flew in the face of her grandfather's concerns, it was nevertheless those words' implicit sense of urgency that Allison would cherish as the inspiration for her actions. He was right. Time was quick. Too quick to take for granted. Too quick to resist the notion that snuck into her head and took root. By the time the first glow of dawn had lightened the sleepless shadows of her bedroom (the same bedroom that had been hers as a child), she knew she simply had to give it a try.

~1987~

The most important singing lesson Allison Page ever received from the great Margaret Calloway took place when she was only 12 years old, barely a month after the two began meeting twice a week to attend to the tasks of scales and breathing exercises, vowel-shaping and diction. Indeed it oc-curred only after the fruits of those labours had ripened gloriously for the entire audience of the public school's Spring Fling Variety Concert, during which her nervous and fidgety young frame had risen to tiptoe up to the stage, and with a theretofore unknown crystal-clear voice had reduced the auditorium full of teachers, parents and townsfolk to a unison of sobs with a selection from *Les Misérables* (of the classroom music teacher's, not Maggie's, choosing). The lesson came mere moments afterwards, in fact, with young Allison – despite her accomplishment – slumped on the top tier of her school's now-empty music room, heaving her own tears into the fur-trimmed lapel of Maggie's coat. The lesson, in fact, had nothing whatsoever to do with the technique that those initial weeks of training had tried to instill, nor with the performance she had just delivered. It did, however, have everything to do with music.

■

It had taken an outsider to break down the barriers that had built up around Ms. Calloway's reclusiveness. Someone not privy to the whispers and gossip of the local musical community – those that painted the picture of a bitter, selfish woman more content to sit in her country house amongst the memorabilia of her accomplished career, than stoop to share her talents with the harsh vowel sounds and wandering pitch of mere amateurs. True, in the beginning these same whisperers were the voice of unbounded optimism, so overjoyed were they with the news that upon Ms. Calloway's sudden retirement she had decided to purchase her childhood home and return to the shores of Georgian Bay, where she had been raised. But after five years of unrequited appeals from school music programs and community choirs alike, the once-constant cascade of overtures had all but dripped dry, and the once-highly-publicized fact that a world-famous concert soprano was a native daughter was no longer proclaimed from the lips of anyone in the town's music circles.

Fortunately for Allison, her grandfather, in his beleaguered state of semi-retirement (the *semi* aspect having been necessitated by the sudden financial burden of an unexpected 10-year-old dependent) was in no way a part of these circles and therefore paid no attention to the sorts who over coffee at a lunch counter or in line at the grocer's might talk of Ms. Calloway in disparaging tones.

His job was to help run the town's arena – open the doors every 8:00 a.m., mop the floors, stock the concession counter, maintain the ice and do the books – then come home and look after his granddaughter. His only memory of Maggie Calloway was from the one-room school back at Big Bay, where she had been two grades behind him … three rows over, one seat up. He did remember saving her toque one day from a pack of rather menacing teenage girls who had been quite determined to steal it away from someone who, in their minds, was simply too different to leave be. But apart from that incident, Maggie Calloway was just a name that Helen would come across from time to time, whenever the paper had something in about her travelling to this country and that, singing her concerts.

Murray Page missed his wife terribly. Missed every single detail about her. But in the midst of his mourning her sudden passing – diagnosed with pancreatic cancer on a cold January afternoon and gone a mere six months later – Allison had come along. And with her had come added regret to mix with his grief; regret that the order of the tragedies that had befallen his family had been nothing short of cruel. If only Helen had been there for at least some of Allison's childhood. In so many instances, she would have known so much better what to do. But she was four months buried by the time the girl's mother lost control of the car that slippery November day. And when Allison's father, Murray Jr., suddenly packed up three weeks after that, without so much as a word of explanation – just one brief call a week later to say he was out in Edmonton with friends, would send some cash when he could but wouldn't be coming home – it all fell on Murray's aging shoulders to try to carry on.

It wasn't easy. The succession of losses had effectively shut his grand-daughter down. She continually balked at having classmates over to play, and when Murray tried to invoke his will to rectify the matter the results were nothing short of disastrous. Allison spent the bulk of her 11th birthday party cross-legged, rocking in the shadows of her bedroom, while a half-dozen girls – taken from a class list after a great struggle of deliberation by her schoolteacher – played unconcerned on the front lawn. Similarly when babysitters came – a frequent occurrence through the winter, as Murray often had to work late at the arena – she would retire to the solemn refuge of her room where she would later be found by her grandpa, asleep amongst dozens of scattered pages from her sketch pad. And seeing her there, safe in her one and only refuge (unsuitable though it was for an 11-year-old girl's tastes, its orange and brown wallpaper and the dark, tightly-drawn chestnut drapes both holdovers from his late wife's decorating), he would gather the sheets of pictures she had rendered – always a variation of the same scene … some body of water, be it river or a lake, with a boat somewhere in the foreground, and tall craggy mountains off in the distance – and he would place them carefully in her bedside drawer on top of those from the previous night. Then he would retire to his easy chair with a cup of tea, where he would stare into the evening news and lament tragedy's order all over again.

It was actually Allison's art teacher who first noticed the quiet but content melodies slipping from the girl's lips whenever she drew or painted in class. She mentioned it to Allison's homeroom teacher, who in turn spoke about it to a by-then-desperate Murray Page during a parent-teacher interview, suggesting that some aptitude and interest, perhaps, lay in singing. Knowing the name of only one "singing person", Murray jumped into the cab of his black Ford pickup and, with an ignorance that cleverly disguised itself as guile, drove directly to the home of Ms. Maggie Calloway, world-renowned soprano and former student of the Big Bay one-room school – three rows over, one seat up.

She had barely opened her front door, when he started in on an impromptu plea to take on his granddaughter for singing lessons, completely oblivious to the fact that Maggie Calloway had for the past five years shown absolutely no interest in sharing her musical expertise with anyone. Yet after his brief appeal had run its course – in the silent space between inquiry and response, where Ms. Calloway traditionally replied that she was under no obligation to assist in any local musical endeavours because, contrary to the wishes of her neighbours, she was truly *retired* (and here she would invariably stress this word a bit beyond the measure of politeness) – a one-and-only-one exception took place. And it was the exception which would launch the sequence of events that would lead directly to Allison Page's most important singing lesson.

"Well, what's it gonna be?" Murray asked, once the silence had lingered beyond his liking.

The elderly woman cocked her head to the side rather quizzically, and with a recording of some music that the man had never heard before in his life playing on the stereo behind her, gave her response.

"You saved my hat, didn't you?"

■

Maggie Calloway lived all alone in a large stone house overlooking Georgian Bay. It stood well back from the road, at the end of a long meandering lane that curved like a dusty ribbon between the sun-soaked scrub of the homestead's now-retired fields where the bulk of her father's farm had once been cleared, in the sweeping rise of grasses that sloped up from the property's fenceline to a crown of open terrain. The house was framed by the barn to the west, and the orchard in behind. The orchard was followed by one last small field, then the woods, all the way to the base of the cliff – the Niagara Escarpment, to visiting hikers. Skinner's Bluff if you were local.

It was a beautiful old home, rather regal in its simplicity. Two storeys, with a gable off the front, weathered and paled from the wind and climate that had beaten against it for over a century, but still standing strong in the face of time. And while the drawn drapes, the somewhat dull greens and browns of the neglected flower beds, and the chipped-paint picket fence may not have been inviting to many, to the shy young girl with a penchant for shadows it instantly offered something intriguing. A vantage perhaps. For the very moment she emerged from her grandpa's truck that first afternoon, her eyes were captured by the panorama of the fields stretching out from the comfortable stone of the farmhouse and back toward the road from which they had come. She was entranced by how the land rolled out and away from her, bathed in the late-day sun, back down the lane, out past the road, right out to the distant rich deep blue of the bay. It was a view better than she had ever imagined, a view better than she had ever tried to draw. And it was a view that would enchant more with each and every visit. In winter or summer. Cloud or sunlight. From the veranda or the orchard fence. Even from the second-storey bedroom window where Maggie once found the girl, despite her "music room only" regulations regarding their lessons. The same bedroom where Maggie had spent her own childhood, she later confided – a childhood no doubt spent, Allison imagined, sitting on the sill, staring out at the vast rich vista of field and shore and endless blue horizon, dreaming of the star she would one day become. In time this would become Allison's own private thesis regarding her mentor. That all of Maggie's travels, all of her exploits, all her successes ... all somehow owed their entitlement to this limitless view.

On her initial visit, however, Allison had no need to stray past the music room, taking it in fully and methodically, only vaguely aware of the speech Ms. Calloway was directing towards her. Something about the need to work hard and heed all instruction if their association was to bear even the most modest of rewards ... she didn't get it all on the first pass, preoccupied as she was with the room's details. The huge oak shelves full of records and sheet music. The dark polished grand piano. The ornately carved wooden music stand, a dictation book at the ready on its easel, with Allison's name printed neatly on top. The far wall adorned with photographs of a younger, slimmer woman, often in performance, one of her holding a large bouquet of roses, one of her shaking hands with a conductor. She took in all of it, in a silent slow arc around the room until she had come full circle, finding herself staring out a huge picture window, once again in front of the view which would be her audience for the next several years of singing lessons; and the view of countless visits for years after that.

She stared out the window undaunted, unconcerned. Past the wind-whipped grasses. Past the deep blue unconfined water. Stared as far as she could see … and then for the first time in her short disrupted life, stared a little further …

… and hummed a little tune.

●

Distress Line. This is Jason.

    – Is Andrew there? Andrew 03?

Hey Eli, Buddy, how's the world of choral music?

    – Andrew?

Nope; 'fraid you got me tonight, My Man.

    – I have to talk to Andrew.

You do?

    – Yes. About the concert.

Are we talking the Emerson Place opening again?

    – Yes, yes. Today is February 1st.

Is that important, Eli?

    – Of course it's important! Damn it, there's only eight weeks until we open.

So what's the problem?

    – What's the problem, he asks!

Hey, sorry, Man–

> – *It's the bloody acoustics of course! They won't be able to support the dynamics!*

The dynamics?

> – *Yes. Yes. The dynamics. The Louds. The Softs. Forte. Pianissimo. High and low frequencies.*

Yeah I'm with you, Eli, but wouldn't –

> – *The orchestra's dynamic range as a whole is far greater than that of any choir, let alone a solo voice. The architecture needs to respect that. Right from the low string bass lines to the high winds and the trumpet passages. It all has to be part of the equation. That's why the orchestra is physically pitted below the level of the choir. That's why you elevate the voices of those singing. But those can't be the only considerations or else we could go hear the* Messiah *at any old school auditorium with raised bleachers, couldn't we?*

Well I'm no expert, Eli, but I doubt the engineers and the architects would have gone ahead and built some 800-seat concert hall–

> – *Try two thousand and fifty-six.*

Two thousand and fifty-six it is. My point is, they're probably not going to build the thing without consulting, you know ... some expert on acoustics.

> – *No, you're still not listening. Don't you understand? It's too late for all that. The side walls are insufficiently curved. The acoustic deflection too gradual for – Ah Christ you don't get it at all. Where the hell is Andrew ... I need to talk to Andrew, goddamn it!*

Eli, Buddy ... I told you. There's no one named–

> – *Yeah, yeah ... 'No one named Andrew' ... goddamn it (click)*

•

The pair of tear-soaked eyes emerged from the woman's coat.

"So, Allison, tell me," the woman commanded as she adjusted her gloves in what seemed a deliberate disregard for the girl's emotional state. "How do you think you did tonight?"

Allison paused to consider an answer, moving her gaze to a silver brooch that was clamped to the left collar of the woman's coat. She tried a muffled word or two of what she thought would be the proper tone of self-evaluation, but then succumbed to another round of uncontrolled sobs and collapsed back into the woman's lap, which was awkward, for Maggie Calloway had never been one particularly skilled in the art of consolation. With hands raised – as if some cold drink had just been spilled on her finery – she slowly slid herself out from under the crying child, then fumbled to subdue her young student's hands between the palms of her own, so she could deposit and pin them back in the girl's lap.

"Let's try again," she said matter-of-factly, as she smoothed out a few offending rumples in the girl's dress. "How do you think you performed this evening?"

"… no good at all," she managed weakly.

"No good?"

Allison shook her head.

"… at all?"

She shook her head harder and sniffed back the residue of the past few minutes' tears.

"Well that is interesting. I mean a soloist should always be mature in her own assessments, but from what I heard tonight, everything we worked on … your tone and your breathing … you incorporated these things quite well into your piece. And surely you heard the applause. The audience was obviously quite taken with you. Yet strangely, you say you were no good at all."

"Well at least ... not good enough."

"Not good enough? For whom? For me?" More head shaking and a fresh round of tears. "I certainly hope that's not it, because you should not be up there on a stage only to please me, Young Lady. Yes, you should take my advice and heed my instruction, but when it comes to motivation and the desire to sing to your fullest potential, well that must all come from within. So if you are labouring here under the assumption that I was some-how displeased with the way you sang–"

"She already said it's not you." The voice came from the doorway over the woman's shoulder where Murray Page, in his twice-a-year suit, stood awkwardly, unsure whether to proceed into the room or hold his ground where he was. Murray too was not one strong on consoling.

"It's that deadbeat father o' hers," he explained from across the room. "She wrote him letters about this concert. Half a dozen or more. Told him how she'd been picked to sing a solo. Sent them off to different friends' ad-dresses where we thought somebody might know his whereabouts. Some of 'em came back 'return to sender'. But a couple didn't, so while we nev-er got a reply ... I think Allison hoped there was a chance he'd be proud enough ... man enough ..."

His words trailed off and though his emotion was a much quieter ver-sion than his granddaughter's, its power still bade him retreat to the hallway to collect himself while Allison once again collapsed back on her teacher, her face this time swallowed up by the generous mink trim of the woman's coat. Once again Maggie took the child by the wrists and raised the tiny body off her. This time, however, she pulled the girl up to her own face.

"I need to tell you why we sing," she stated quietly, after a prolonged scrutiny of the youngster, with a hint of a smile that Allison could not remember ever seeing before. "Or at the very least I need to tell you why we *should* sing. And please note when I say *we* I don't mean this is why everyone sings, or that this is some golden rule of the stage. Lord knows the world's concert halls have seen more than their share of heartless technicians, mimicking the wishes of grand composers to thunderous ovations." The smile disappeared. "Regurgitating notes and musical direction with all the precision of a can opener. Sadly, all the passion of one too. Trust me, Young Lady, I've seen entire careers go by that never managed to grasp what I am about to tell you."

She pushed herself up from the classroom's terraced floor and stood tall and straight before the still-limp child, her hands folded neatly together in front of her.

"Allison," she addressed, wanting to be certain of the girl's attention. "Allison?"

"What?"

"Is what your grandfather said true? Were you hoping your performance here tonight would bring your father back?"

Allison shrugged and worked to avoid her teacher's gaze, glancing this way and that, off toward the doorway, the window, up to the ceiling. She didn't want to talk about it. She just wanted to forget the whole thing. The letters. The singing lessons. The whole stupid thing. She wished she had never let her grandpa talk her into going to Ms. Calloway's in the first place. Wished she had never seen that stupid music room with that stupid view of the bay. She wanted to go home. She wanted to be in her dark bedroom again. Alone. Alone was her only real friend. She could always count on Alone.

"Allison, I asked you a question," Maggie repeated. "Did you think your father would come back to hear you sing–"

"YES!" she exploded, surprising herself how loud and sudden her anger had arrived. But before she could regroup to apologize, or bolt from the room, or indeed exercise an option on any possible follow-up to the outburst, the woman in front of her – the woman who did not console –

lowered herself back down beside the girl and, quietly, asked Allison to sit up straight and look her in the eye.

"Then your assessment was correct. Your singing tonight was clearly not good enough."

Allison stared at her teacher blankly and a grunt of protest filtered in from the hallway. "Do you know why I say this, Allison?"

She shook her head.

"Because no one's singing would be good enough. Yours. Mine. Pavarotti's. No one's." The woman went to work on the wrinkles in the girl's dress once more. "These are hard lessons that fate has thrown at you, Allison. And at such a young age. But I will not trifle with the truth. And the truth in this matter, quite simply, is that no one's talent could have accomplished what you were asking of yours here tonight."

"I know," the girl relented, slapping the sides of her legs as she rose and paced a little. "It was stupid!"

"I didn't say that," the woman cut in quickly, rising to join Allison in her walk about the room. "In fact, if you want to know something?" she continued. "You remind me a little of myself when I was young. Well ... maybe a little older. Fourteen perhaps? I had won a local singing competition, you see ... right down the street in the old Anglican Church hall, in fact. Not that it was a monumental achievement, seeing as it was the fourth time my mother had entered me and there were never more than a half-dozen singers in any one year. Nevertheless, my prize was a trip to the Royal Winter Fair to sing in a provincial competition with other young vocalists from all around Ontario, and my mother was, shall we say, quite diligent in making sure I did not arrive at the event unprepared. I can still remember the day. I wore a pink taffeta dress with tiered panels on the skirt and a white lace collar, a matching ribbon for my hair. And if you believe my mother's version of events, I sang my test piece more purely and clearly than anyone there, by far. *I Know My Redeemer Liveth*. It's an aria from Handel's *Messiah*.

"Unfortunately for Mother, an older girl from Listowel took first place. Millicent Meredith. For some reason, I can still remember her name. And her prize. There was a stipend to be used towards lessons – but much more impressively, a large trophy and a blue flowered hat that was the envy of everyone there. For my second-place efforts, I was given a small silver medallion in a cherrywood case that would have looked quite nice on top of the family piano, had Mother not removed it from sight immediately upon our return. She was convinced the judging had been unfairly biased towards the taller curly-haired Millicent, you see. Especially since two of the three adjudicators were young men from the University whose young ears, so my mother claimed, had been impaired by her beguiling smile. And as for their adjudicators' notes regarding my performance as being 'laudable but perhaps not a prudent choice of music for such a young innocent voice', well let's just say that particular piece of paper did not survive the trip home."

Maggie sat back down and sighed. "It was a pretty little thing, that medallion. Such a shame Mother's fuss overshadowed it so, stomping from the hall the way she did, leaving me to just sit there while she chased around the organizers and demanded justice. But I guess I should be thankful in a way, because while she was busy with all of that, Millicent's mother, of all people, came over and spoke the words that I want you to hear now, Allison."

The young girl stopped her back-and-forth, the first sign of any real curiosity for the woman's story.

"She sat down, smiled at me – quite a genuine smile mind you – and she said, 'You just can't compete, can you, Dear?' Now I'm sure she realized immediately from the incredulous look on my face that she had chosen her words poorly, because she instantly started apologizing. 'Oh no, no Dear, please don't misunderstand.' She was waving her hands and patting my hair. 'I didn't mean *you* can't compete. Why, I thought you and Millicent and all the others sang so beautifully today.' And that's when I first noticed that she didn't quite look like my mother, nor any of the other mothers in attendance. She didn't dress as they did. She didn't wear her clothes as proudly. Didn't carry herself with the same – well, I'll say grace but really that's too flattering – self-importance is probably the more accurate term. 'This is all so new for Millicent and me,' she said. 'Millicent's school insisted she should have singing lessons, so we took her to our choir director at the church and he worked with her some and, well, here we are. It's just too bad that he decided not to come. You see, our choir director is of the opinion that the joy of a melody should be its own reward, not the means to some shiny medal or fancy hat or what have you. And I must say after hearing all your beautiful voices here today, well I may just have to agree. You can't compete. You shouldn't compete. Not when it comes to music.'

"Now I'll confess, Allison, for the next few ambitious years of my life, I gave no credence to this woman whatsoever. In fact, when I told my mother of Mrs. Meredith's conversation later, she regarded it merely as proof of her daughter's inferiority; proof that in our quest for vocal perfection, we would never need deal with the likes of Millicent Meredith ever again; that Millicent and her mother would likely live out their short-sighted lives no closer to glory than the 2nd row of a church choir in some little farm town at the end of the map.

"But the woman spoke the truth, Allison. The simple truth inaccessible to only the stubborn and the proud. And someone who displays such obvious talent as yourself should consider Mrs. Meredith's words carefully. You should know what your talent *won't* be able to accomplish before you set out trying to accomplish it. That way you can better decide whether pursuing that talent is still something you would like to do. Because what you tried to do tonight, Allison, what you hoped for … was impossible. You should not sing to exact rewards from others. Trust me, it just doesn't work like that. Singing can't bring your father back."

Allison considered this in silence a moment, then slapped her sides once more.

"So why even bother then?" she blurted out, once again more suddenly than she had intended.

Maggie waved the girl over, patting the floor beside her, and Allison sat down.

"The answer, My Dear, is right there in your question. You should sing precisely *because* you can't bring your father back. Or your mother. You should sing because music and lyrics translate feelings you otherwise can't express. And then you should sing to share those feelings with others. Others whose emotions are just as deep, but for whatever reason have not the clarity of tone to voice them. You should sing so they can borrow that from you."

Maggie gingerly lifted herself up from the step. "I'll tell you what," she offered. "You take until the end of the school year to think about all this … Mr. Page?" She called over her shoulder and Allison's grandfather returned to the doorway.

"Mr. Page, your granddaughter is going to take some time to determine whether the reasons for singing are worth the effort. Isn't that right, Allison?"

With a nod, the young girl agreed she would do just that, though clearly, even then, she already knew her answer.

"But if so?" the woman added, the slight grin returning to her face once more. "No more show tunes. Yuck."

~DECEMBER 11, 2010~

Finally the house lights dimmed and the conductor arrived, his commanding presence – tall and lean with jet-black curly hair – compelling the audience into an instant wave of unsolicited applause as he strode across the stage and up onto his podium. With the power of but a finger and the tip of a baton, he readied the orchestra for its opening foray.

Allison took the opportunity to risk her first lengthy glance past Maggie to the seat beyond, noting how the contribution to that opening applause from the woman seated there had been slight at best. Four claps and then back to checking on something in her handbag, which she then tucked neatly and carefully behind the back of her knee. Next she pulled the already perfectly-straight collar of her blazer straighter, smoothed her already well-pressed skirt smoother, squared her shoulders, folded her arms and settled in for the evening with a muted yet betraying sigh. All of which served to chase Allison's thoughts back to the woman's initial opinion about the evening at hand.

■

"What in God's name are you thinking? All the way to Toronto. For one bloody concert? Have you gone completely insane? Have you?" The volley had begun as soon as Allison had picked up the receiver, having been paged from her Grade 9 woodwinds class to take an urgent *family* message.

"My mother is not a plaything for your amusement and for you to completely disregard her many serious health issues for the sake of this … this hare-brained notion …"

It was obvious by the questioning looks from the secretarial staff that the caller's volume was easily seeping past Allison's ear and into the office at large. She mouthed a plaintive "I'm sorry" to Mrs. Grishwald, who had taken the call, smiling weakly when she noticed the secretary ironically mouthing back the very same thing.

Allison Page had never met her voice teacher's daughter when she was growing up. In fact she could not remember her name being mentioned even casually in conversation at all. Nor could she recall any references by Maggie about her husband, not that the absence of a Mr. Calloway in

Maggie's house had ever concerned her. Eventually – through a quiet but persistent local rumour mill – she would learn that the marriage had failed many years before. But it would not be until Allison returned as an adult that she would know anything further, though it would be nothing of any great detail and certainly nothing intended.

It happened on one of their Saturday afternoon visits when the elder woman had excused herself to fetch a refill of lemon for their tea – always lemon for the voice, she maintained, even in her retirement. She had returned to find Allison leafing through an old cardboard box of unframed photos that usually stayed high atop a shelf in her hallway's end closet, but had been momentarily brought out from the shadows that morning during some spring cleaning. Their proximity had proved irresistible and Allison had quickly lost herself in the stacks of pictures, most showing old performances, fellow soloists or favoured conductors; many included a well-wish scrolled in the lower corner from the person pictured. But below them was one that was most intriguing. There was a young woman and a strappingly tall and refined man walking behind a pram with a toddler sitting proudly up from within, a knitted cap pulled tightly down over her head on what appeared to be a cold crisp winter morning. *Maggie and Russ Cochrane with baby Christine. Christmas 1958* read the caption in the bottom corner. Allison remembered fingering the tattered rolled-up corners of the picture, staring at the faded yellow image. Such a happy little family. Such a sad little photo.

But Allison never questioned her friend about it. Not then, nor any time later. She understood only too well that sometimes anguish was better left unframed and undisplayed. She didn't need to know specifics. Not at the expense of that anguish. They had their music after all. And it was music at a depth that surpassed any unnecessary conversation about their own feeble and fallible conditions, their failures or their losses, their doctor's appointments and their ultrasounds, their painful childhoods, their issues of abandonment, their failed loves; their un-lived lives. No, they had their music. One afternoon a week to swim melodically through the silent depths of their emotions and be strangely free of them all at the same time. Their music and their tea. That was enough.

"Look – you have truly spun my poor mother's head completely around with this idea of yours. Toronto is a three-hour trip each way. She hasn't done a drive like that in years. Years! What if something goes amiss? What if there's a health emergency out on the highway? And then there's the weather. Am I to simply put the trust of my mother's welfare in your hands? Yes, I know you have had wonderful times with Mother since you moved back. And yes, I do count you among her closest friends. Trust me, I hear all about your Saturday afternoons time and time again. But therein again lies the problem, doesn't it, Allison? Surely you have noted how often Mother is repeating herself these days. How easily she gets confused."

Of course she had noticed. She was the first to notice. The confusion, the repetition, the shortness of breath. But weren't these conditions the very reasons for their trip in the first place? It was now or never. Couldn't the heartless hag see that?

She seethed all the way home from school that afternoon, her anger having grown to entertain a litany of cutting rebuttals she wished she could have accessed at the time of the call. Such was Allison's way, her best lines delivered in the safety of her own conscience, and not in the heat of the debate. And so, predictably, the response that did reach Christine's ears was far less forceful.

"I just thought it might be something she would enjoy."

"Did you?"

"She just still loves her Handel so much–"

"Yes, Allison. I'm well aware of the musical tastes of my own mother."

"And I'm sorry. I didn't mean to overstep my bounds."

"And yet clearly that is exactly what you have done, isn't it? Was I informed of this excursion when it was being planned? No. Not a word of it until the nurse casually mentions it last night on the phone."

"You're upset."

"You're damned right I'm upset. When it appears someone is trying to amuse themselves at the expense of my mother's well-being ... surprise! I am going to be upset."

■

Without moving the angle of her head Christine shot an irritated look over to Allison's lost gaze, causing her to avert her eyes quickly back towards the conductor just in time for his opening dramatic gesticulation – arms suddenly outstretched and circling upward as if he were actually trying to gather up the entire orchestra and hold it aloft. Then, just as suddenly, down swooped his arms to his sides and with them came forth the first grand notes from the strings.

For all her eager anticipation of this moment, its actual arrival found the young schoolteacher elsewhere – preoccupied not with the downbeat, but instead with the possibility that perhaps the bored woman two seats over had been destined to become the woman she was, that she had suffered from her mother's shadow. Granted, at first glance, from her designer wardrobe to her perfectly set and coloured hair, her careful makeup and diligently manicured nails, it would be hard to imagine. And then there was the lineage that her marriage into the Avery family – as in Avery's Mutual Insurance of Waterloo – had bestowed upon her, placing her well in that city's and indeed the province's circle of the advantaged. Her husband Mike's father and grandfather had both sat on the boards of the university there and both had taken terms in public office, his father as mayor, his grandfather as Member of Parliament. She and her husband enjoyed a highly successful marriage. (Allison had actually heard Christine describe it in those terms one day while on the phone to someone during one of her whirlwind trips to the farm to check on her mother's caregivers.) She was a patron of the arts, donating regularly to regional orchestras, choral societies, the theatre in Stratford. Yet these efforts, as with her wardrobe and hair and nails, all seemed to be measured out with complete reserve, in keeping, Allison decided just as the violins led off the second passage of the overture, with someone whose concerns about lining up her handbag behind her knee superseded the actual performance she was there to hear. A decidedly arm's-length appreciation. Not too high. Not too low. Just so.

Had it always been that way? Had music, for this offspring of musical genius, never held any more depth than mere propriety's sake? Surely there was a time – a time of innocent youth perhaps – when young Christine would have lain awake at night, her imagination well outdistancing some imposed bedtime schedule. Surely she would have concocted stories and tales of rich fantasy as she lay in some cozy stone-walled bedroom, warmly adorned with a bed and canopy, cocooned beneath well-stuffed duvets and deep plush pillows – a family flat back in London perhaps   with a view of Tudor houses … row upon row of thatched roofs … unrealistic certainly, but Allison didn't care. These were her fantasies, and she could decorate them any way she saw fit. A quaint stone cottage tucked into a small cobbled street perhaps. The home from which they would make their visits to grand concert halls with rich velvet curtains and vivid tapestries … halls where Mommy rehearsed and performed and was treated with the importance of a queen. And lying there against such a backdrop would Christine not have finally drifted off digesting the tones of scales and exercises, the repetition of soaring melodies that came wafting under an old oak door from the drawing-room where her mother would practise long into the night? Perhaps asking that the big oak door be left slightly ajar so that a sliver of light and music could keep her company until sleep finally came. Allison simply could not imagine such a childhood in any other manner. And yet clearly such was not the stuff of Christine's upbringing. The person named

Mother – certainly *Mom* or *Mama* seemed out of the question, given the way both women carried themselves – did not appear to have ever been her daughter's mentor or guide. Perhaps, Allison reluctantly allowed, Maggie's influence upon her child owed more to a remote parenthood, with constant interruptions for concert tours and promotional excursions. Interruptions that left the child alone with a father who, according to Maggie's one and only account of the man – uttered absently as she had grabbed the one and only family picture and thrown it back in its box, then thrown the box back in its dark hall closet – had the singular skill of being *remote* while sitting in the very next chair. And if this had been the case, perhaps such influence had destined Christine to a life that would be decidedly not musical, leaving in that void nothing but the need to search elsewhere for self-importance on the scale her mother had once enjoyed. Whatever the case, one thing was abundantly clear. Maggie and her daughter were not, and had never been, close. The tail end of that angry call to school had already confirmed as much.

"Christine. Please believe me. I am only thinking of your mother's well-being. I think it would be so meaningful for her to go back and visit the stage where she gave her final performance–"

"You mean the stage where she suddenly decided to end her career. Emerson Place, please. Did it ever occur to you that my mother may not wish to revisit that over-glorified slab of concrete?"

"Well, she seemed excited when we talked about it–"

"It's her confusion talking, My Dear. Nothing more. And I would bet a year's wages that if you spelled out clearly where you wanted to take her you'd see a far different response. But then again, I doubt you have even ever bothered to ask why my mother walked off that stage twenty-eight years ago and promptly retired."

Allison was fumbling for words now. "No … I mean … I wasn't comfortable prying into something that didn't feel open for discussion."

"Didn't feel like prying. Really? Clearly, you seem to be making up for it."

"Christine, come on. I just assumed that all the years of travel and touring had caught up with her and she was burned out."

There was a pause on the other end, a pause that served as prelude to a modicum of acquiescence and probably facilitated the hasty negotiations that ensured the trip could continue, for the most part, as planned, on the condition that Christine herself meet them in Toronto and be on hand to 'monitor the state' of her mother's condition throughout the evening.

"Well of course she was tired out. She spent her life out there onstage," came the calmer, quieter reply. And in the echo of that subdued tone Allison suddenly realized, without the slightest doubt, that when it came to the motives behind the great Maggie Calloway's sudden decision to quit singing, her own daughter had no idea either.

●

Distress Line. This is Jason.
    – *Hello?*
Eli, is that you again?
    – *I'm sorry I got angry and hung up on you.*
That's OK, but I really have to move on to other calls, OK Buddy?
    – *Do you know anything about Handel's* Messiah?
I know it gets you worked up.
    – *I'm sorry.*
Kind of a love-hate relationship you have going there.
    – *Yes.*
You think you should do something about that, Eli?

– Yes. I will. I promise. Good night
OK. Good night, Eli.

●

With the final yearning notes of the overture drawn across the low strings he reaches the far end of the orchard. The dog is well ahead now, her pawprints dotting a haphazard pattern of freedom into the smooth clean snow. His path, by contrast, remains awkwardly steadfast … the shortest line between himself and his destination.

Soon that firm clear minor chord will ring off almost to silence, with only its bare remnants left to modulate subtly the line into the major. Then the tenor will rise from his chair poised to project the oratorio's very first words – words attributed to no less than the very Mouth of God …

Comfort ye. Comfort ye my people

And he will be off again, through the last remaining field that rises up the hill before giving way to the untamed wilderness beyond. His shoulders will be hunched into the chill of the stiffening wind. His arms will be folded tightly to his body. His head down. His eyes frozen to the ground directly ahead of his feet. He will observe little. He will discover nothing.

Recitative:
Comfort Ye ...

At the first sight of Kyle, Peter jumped up and pushed out an available chair.

"I'm late ... Sorry," his date puffed out. "Class ran late. I see you have the tickets already."

"Row C. Seats 4 and 5. And don't sound so disappointed."

"Did I say anything?"

"You had a look."

"Well you know, I just got thinking on the way over what a shame it would be not to take advantage of this warm weather, out here in the open air, sipping drinks on a patio."

"You're kidding, right?"

"We should take advantage of it while we can, shouldn't we? I mean today – April 1st, 1982 – is bound to go down as the warmest on record. Do we really want to tell everyone we spent it in some dark stuffy concert hall?"

"No really, tell me you're joking."

"Surely you felt that warm breeze on your walk down here."

"Actually I drove."

"Oh Peter."

"I know, I know. But it was already a quarter to five ..."

"So I am late then."

Peter grinned sheepishly. "No ... me early," he shrugged. "I'm just excited, that's all."

"So you are," Kyle responded with a smile, and leaned in to rest his hand on top of Peter's.

"Careful there, Boyfriend."

"Public proximity?"

"Public proximity," he repeated, revisiting in his mind the Sunday brunch up on College Street when they had first come up with the phrase, seated between two families of screaming children and scowling parents. "Oops, Mama's scared for her young 'uns," Peter had whispered – probably a bit too loudly – just as the mother of a free-range toddler in full strawberry-jam face paint plucked up her child and pinned him on her lap with all the strength her family values could summon.

"Thanks for inviting me," Kyle said, swiftly releasing his touch. "And yes, I was just pulling your chain."

"Ooh, promises, promises."

"Down, Boy," his friend said, with a roll of the eyes. "You have work to do. You have exactly ..." Kyle checked his watch, "an hour and a half to educate me, oh Pundit of Classical Music. So ... Handel's *Messiah*. What should I expect?"

"What should you expect?" Peter repeated to himself, momentarily scanning the skyline as he searched for a proper answer. "Well, for one thing," he began, his grin turning slightly mischievous, "you should expect tonight to be the start of an excellent tradition for us. Yes?"

"Let's just walk before we run, OK , Maestro?"

"I swear, Kyle, it won't be like last time."

"Peter, you know I am truly interested in the things that interest you. But after that fiasco of an opera, I retain all rights to my own opinions, thank you very much."

"Fine ... good. But aren't you curious why I would make such a declaration?"

"I am not."

"Because I am confident that the powers of George Frideric and Charles Jennens will win you over."

"Who?"

"Charles Jennens. He's the librettist."

"What's that, the words guy?"

It was Peter's turn to roll his eyes. "Yes, Kyle ... the words guy."

"But you said this thing–"

"This *thing*?" he winced.

"Well whatever you call it ... it's not an opera. Oh God, Peter, tell me it's not another opera."

"Relax, you philistine."

"Because you promised–"

"It's an oratorio."

"An oratorio, right," Kyle repeated. "And what is that, exactly?"

"It is essentially a narrative set to music without a dramatic staging."

"And you said this one is based on the Bible."

"Well, it is called the *Messiah*, Einstein. But someone still had to choose and compile and organize which passages were going to be used, right? I mean it's not like we're going to sit through the singing of the whole Bible from cover to cover–"

"This is my fear ..."

"So Jennens picked the scriptural passages that best conveyed the central story of ... well ... the Messiah. And just for the record, from all I've read and researched, the honour went straight to his over-inflated head. Did you know the egotistical old git actually critiqued Handel's score?"

"I could say I did, but, clearly, I'd be lying."

"It's true. There's a quote in one of the companion books I picked up. Apparently he found the opening music of the overture, and I quote, 'unworthy of Handel and far more unworthy of the Messiah Himself'. The blowhard. I mean, what credentials did he have to make a statement like that? Over-glorified stalker, if you ask me. Probably ran around London chasing Handel down until he agreed to use one of his librettos."

"That sounds rude."

"Handel probably agreed just to get him off his ass."

"Still rude."

"I think Townsend had it right, though. He said the overture was 'like great billows of the ocean'. And do you know why?"

"Hey, I didn't even know who the Jansen guy—"

"Jennens."

"Sorry."

Peter chose to ignore the growing smirk emerging from the corner of his friend's mouth, and with a quick lubricating gulp of ale pressed on undaunted. "Because Townsend understood that this divine work lost all of its divinity if it was chopped up and dissected music-from-word, word-from-music. But I'm getting ahead of myself. So to answer your question—"

"What was my question? I forgot."

"What you can expect. So here it is. The concert will be split into three parts. The first covers the prophecy of a Saviour right up until His birth. The second is His life and death. The third is His resurrection."

"Sounds long."

"Come on, Kyle."

"I'm kidding. The non-music major is making a bit of a joke. By the way, which is our waiter?"

Peter swivelled round and waved at a tall figure balancing several plates of food on a forearm. "Simon ... in the blue," he replied, and picked up his beer bottle, waving the label and two fingers in the man's direction.

"OK, what else do I need to know?"

"Well the oratorio also consists of three different vocal elements. First, and most dramatically, are the choruses."

"Like the Hallelujah Chorus?"

"That's the one everyone knows."

"Even your uncultured little philistine of a boyfriend."

"Shush," Peter returned, with a cuff on the wrist. "The choruses are the full production. Tonight you'll hear them sung by a huge 200-voice choir with full orchestra accompaniment."

"Should be loud enough to keep me awake, anyway."

"And it's nothing compared to some of the nineteenth-century productions that the English concert societies staged. It got to be kind of a pissing contest for rival cities, I think. Choirs of two thousand or more. Orchestras of five hundred musicians. Big and bold, but also pretty cumbersome to keep together."

"Hmm. So size really doesn't–"

"Anyway ..." Peter cut in. "The choruses are the ear candy that first sells people on Handel, and I trust they will blow you away–"

"But I sense there's more?"

"There is, indeed more. Thank you. There are the soloists. First they'll be singing *recitatives* and *accompagnatos*, which are these brief passages that introduce the textual themes of a given cycle within the oratorio as a whole. They're short ... just a few bars really, and they're usually followed by the third element of the oratorio, which is the *aria*. And if you ask me this is where the real enduring beauty of the *Messiah* lies. The arias are these lyrical solos which often continue the narrative of the preceding recitative, but with these beautifully fluid and flowing melodic lines and these repeating phrases that run through a succession of variations on the music."

"Hold the phone ... repeating phrases?"

"It won't seem long, Kyle, I swear. Trust me, there's a reason for the repetition. Just like there's a reason the repeated text is moved through a variety of musical textures. An aria should work like a mantra for your ears. You just have to let it wash over you and let your mind meander."

"Meander?"

"Yes."

"You want me to daydream, Peter?"

"No ... I want you to be lulled. Don't worry. The choruses will always bring you back."

"Lulled?" his young friend mouthed.

"Yes, Kyle, lulled. And speaking of lulled. This beer has lulled my bladder into a false sense of security. Assuming Simon actually shows up with our drinks, can you ask for menus? Oh, and here ... I snagged a copy of the program when I picked up the tickets this morning. Look up who the soloists are tonight."

~DECEMBER 11, 2010~

And the glory of the Lord shall be revealed
And all flesh shall see it together

Maggie Calloway would not revisit any memories of her long and storied career on this night. True, with the soaring first notes of the opening chorus the elderly woman's knuckles had instinctively tightened around the arms of her seat, that particular place in the music, even now, occasioning the same palpable excitement it did when she was the performer – the familiar light twinge in her stomach, the same flutter in her heartbeat arriving like old friends at the very same point they had greeted her all those years ago. This was when she would have begun her silent preparation, when she would have let the performance around her recede, excusing herself – just for an instant – from the thread of the libretto and the artistry of the music, so that she might gather herself and prepare for her own upcoming first entry. Yes, even now, with the woman so frail and dwarfed in her chair, decades removed from her last concert stage, her body answered the music with the same instinctive exercises that had served her so well. First was the even draw of breath which she would lengthen to calm all residual anxiety. ("The day you have no anxiety to calm is the day you should retire," Dr. Blaisdell had always preached.) Next the carefully measured discharge of air done through subtly parted lips and ever-so-slightly flared nostrils so as not to interfere with the elegant poise that was indeed a cornerstone to a successful career. ("You will be seen far sooner than you are heard" was another of Dr. Blaisdell's favourite maxims.)

Poise had not always come easily for Maggie. It had not been a natural commodity. Poise had, in fact, arrived only after years of being instilled. Nailed to her, it had seemed on the worst days. Or at the very least draped on like a heavy garment that would not fit unless she shaped herself to its cut, rather than having it cinched or altered to match her form. But she had persevered, struggling to approximate the diva's role to which she was always told her voice belonged; in the early years as a matter of requirement … in later years, more out of expectation.

How she had wished, on so many occasions, she hadn't needed it so. Needed it to become who she was. She often thought of Neil Raynsford, the affable tenor with whom she had shared the *Messiah* stage on so many occasions, a vocalist every bit as successful as she, and yet with a carefree, laughing spirit that exuded through him right up to and past dress rehearsals, and indeed long after the last notes of the oratorio had died away. She often wondered about Neil. Where retirement had taken him. No doubt, she was sure, to a happy spot. Back to his local pub back in Dublin perhaps. Back to his notorious parties where all gathered around the bar's piano and belted out a few of Handel's louder moments at the top of their lungs "… as God probably just as likely would've preferred," he'd call out in a brogue reserved for private functions, and then chase the moment with a swig of Guinness and with a round of *Christmas in Killarney*, "Just to clear the palate!"

During their touring he had always been the first to lead a post-performance charge to the nearest watering hole. He who had begun each evening a few hours earlier in white tie, with Isaiah's promise that "*Ev'ry valley shall be exalted, and ev'ry mountain and hill made low*", would run around backstage grabbing anyone and everyone – from fellow soloist to viola's last chair – with an egalitarian ease that only his booming gaiety could inspire. But the cloak that was Maggie's constant poise was not so easy, and so she had never accepted any of Neil's invitations. A carefully cultivated career like hers had no room for such impulsiveness. Hers was a life of precise and controlled soaring tones for audiences proper. And any weak moments when she may have allowed herself to entertain the possibility of gathering 'round a public house and belting out a chorus or two were quickly trumped by this understanding. Maggie Calloway was a soprano. Not a tenor.

And yet none of this mattered any more, for it was all well in the unchangeable past, and Maggie Calloway would not be revisiting her past on this night. Not her professional past, at least. Even with Handel's silky phrases now filling her ears, and with her lungs and her breath responding by rote, her mind leapt right past it all. Carnegie Hall, the Sydney Opera House, Emerson Place, the European tours, the tours in the Far East ... the swelling crescendos of applause from well-heeled audiences as she would stride out on stage at the beginning of concerts ... thunderous ovations exploding from the hands of those same patrons at evening's end. The lavish gowns, the endless bouquets, the opulent hotel rooms. The five-star restaurants, the banquets and reception parties, the dinners with royals and heads of state. The tributes and honours, the Order of Canada, the honorary degrees at three separate universities. The six Junos. The two Grammies ... It all just flew by with an unexceptional sameness; a monotony of images in reverse chronology ... back to her earlier years, performances across the prairies ... Calgary, Saskatoon, Brandon ... The bus tours. The motel rooms. The diners ... Her first professional appearance in Kingston, Ontario, not two years removed from her schooling ... until finally, with the choir no more than eight bars in, she landed ... safely and comfortably beyond the point where poise had first conspired against her.

~NOVEMBER 1950~

Until the day he finally spoke to her, she had never noticed him sitting there, alone at the back of the darkened hall. And even then his first words had seemed so quiet and uncertain, a shadow of a voice really.

He had waited until the conclusion of her second of three scheduled full rehearsals, the final preparation before the entire music faculty of Toronto's St. Timothy's College would dare to take on the *Messiah* in public, complete with strings and full choir. Sadly, the run-through, much like the one the week before, had left the poor student soprano with nerves frayed and confidence shaken. True, there had been some improvement. The session had at least survived the first movement, something which could not have been said of the attempt seven days earlier, owing in no small degree to the inexperience and indecisiveness of almost every entry that their young, green soloist had attempted. In fact the conductor had managed to negotiate the production all the way to the end of the oratorio, though he confessed afterwards this had been accomplished more as an exercise of willpower than musicality – accompanying the remark with a long look over his bi-focals towards Maggie, then another towards her vocal coach, one Dr. Enid Blaisdell.

He had also waited until the room had cleared of its tired orchestra and exasperated choristers, and indeed until after Dr. Blaisdell had lifted her sizeable frame from her seat and laboured up onto the stage to where her pupil still stood, dripping with the sweat that had gathered on her cheeks and forehead throughout the three and a half hours she had been there. Waited while she flopped her own copy of music down on a stand she had dragged up behind her then briefly but emphatically went through a lengthy list of details that were still eluding the girl's performance. Pointers regarding technique. About opening more vertical space in her mouth for her soft 'e' vowels, opening up her ahs and bringing the sound forward. Then something about the girl's diction faltering at the end of long phrases. Then a rather firm concluding lecture regarding the need for all of the aforementioned to be automatic in the girl's delivery if her solos were to ever move past the realm of merely a technical exercise and actually start sounding like a performance. Indeed, it was well after the professor had wrapped up with an unenthused "Good night" and trudged away into the now darkened hallway before Maggie first heard his voice at all.

"I think you sounded better tonight."

Maggie's head bobbed up.

"I beg your pardon?" she called out.

"Than last week I mean. You sounded much better."

"Well thank you, but I could hardly have sounded any worse," she replied as her eyes probed the shadows of the hall trying to place the source of both the opinion and the subsequent footsteps, slow and tentative against the hardwood floor.

"I'm sorry if I startled you," he said, finally coming into view about halfway back the centre aisle of the auditorium. "But no one else mentioned that you sounded far better. Probably far better than you think you did."

Maggie examined the awkward-looking young man before her, vaguely recognizing him as someone she may have seen around the college. He was tall but very slight. He wore a dark brown cardigan that hung off him like an overcoat, sagging on the shoulders and with sleeves that drooped over the knuckles of his hands. His face was narrow and pale, his hair thick and dark, and his sad brown eyes peered back at her through a pair of fine wire spectacles.

"Anyway, I just wanted to make sure you knew that," he added with a shrug. "Oh, and I think you should know that when I was sitting back there near some of the music faculty, I could hear them talking. And they were saying all you really have to do is just relax a little bit more ..."

She was truly uncertain how to respond and so for a number of seconds – a great many as far as the boy's nerves were concerned – she said nothing at all, leaving him to fill the awkward silence all on his own, a task he did with such diligence that in short order she had learned a great deal about him. He was not a music major, but rather was studying mathematics. Nevertheless he loved to sit in on orchestra and choir practices at the college because music, he divulged, gave him a warmth that his own studies could not, and the current repertoire she was performing, this *Messiah,* was truly grand. *Grand.* She was intrigued how he had used the word. How he had seemingly chosen it specifically. And when he went on to confess that he knew little about the text, she was strangely impressed again by his use of that term. He had said text. Not lyrics. Not words. *Text.*

Finally, when the boy had rambled through all the information his nervous energy could supply, he shrugged again, nodded quickly and with a quick "Well … goodbye," turned on his heel and made for the hallway.

"So you really just like to come in and listen to rehearsals?"

He stopped and poked his glasses up the bridge of his nose, and by way of an answer, shrugged yet again.

"But why not just come to our performance instead?"

"Oh don't get me wrong. I will. I mean I have … well, on occasion I have. Look I know it's odd, I just prefer the practices better. I like to see how the people create this warmth that I was speaking about. People like yourself … and the orchestra. I guess I'm fascinated by your use of … well, technique I guess you'd say … Technique that creates such feeling." For an instant he thought he detected her mouth move slightly upward in what he allowed himself to believe was a faint smile, but then nerves again quickly intervened. "I'm taking up too much of your time … I'm sorry." And suddenly he was off again for the door.

"No, wait. What's your name?"

From the shadows at the back of the hall she heard his footsteps stop and then his voice, once again quiet.

"Eli … Eli Benowitz."

"So tell me, Eli Benowitz, what have you concluded from observing us here tonight?" she called back. Her voice, she realized, came across like someone trying to sound a little *grand* herself.

For the first time the boy paused to take a sufficiently supported breath before he spoke. "Well," he began slowly, pushing his glasses up the bridge of his nose a second time, then folding his arms tightly in front him, "well from all I've seen and heard here, and from the frown on your face and your conductor's face ... and from the outright scowl on that lady who last spoke with you, I would have to conclude that performing music like this must be ..."

"Nerve-wracking?"

"No. I was going to say serious. It seems very *serious*."

●

You've reached the Distress Line. This is Amy. How can I help you?

— *I want to talk to Andrew.*

Oh hello, Eli. We spoke a few weeks ago.

— *We did?*

We did. We had a very nice chat. You told me all about your love for architecture.

— *I don't love architecture.*

I'm sorry. Maybe that's putting it a little too strongly. Should I have said your interest in architecture? ... hello? Are you still there, Eli?

— *I wouldn't have said that either.*

Well perhaps I'm just not remembering well. I thought we'd had a conversation about the new concert hall going in downtown.

– Emerson Place. Its opening is scheduled for April 1982.

That's right. Only a month away now.

– The first concert will be Handel's Messiah *with the Metropolitan Symphony and the Toronto Chorus under the direction of Walter Engels.*

Oh I know, Eli. I purchased my tickets as soon as they went on sale. They're bringing Neil Raynsford over from Ireland to sing the tenor. And Maggie Calloway's doing the soprano. It should be quite an evening. Tell me, do you like choral music, Eli? … Eli?

– What else did I say?

I beg your pardon?

– The last time. What did I talk about?

Well, like I said, you talked about architecture. And if memory serves, I believe you had some very interesting ideas about the design of buildings and their surroundings.

– I told you about that?

You did, but I must confess it's been a few weeks, so the details are a little foggy. But we have some time now … tell you what, why don't you refresh my memory? Can you do that, Eli?

●

Maggie's friends could not see the attraction. She, of all the voice majors in the college going outside the world to which she aspired, for companionship. After all, there was no shortage of willing and eager suitors right there in the music department. The entire bass section and even a good portion of the tenors – a rather catty alto was wont to mutter – could not help swivelling their heads as one whenever the young woman scurried into choral class (late), her reddish-brown locks blowing behind her as if a spring breeze had decided to attach itself and follow her wherever she went. Why, then, this strange little person with the hunched shoulders and the thick glasses, inquisitive classmates wanted to know. Who was he anyway? Where did he come from?

"He's adopted. To a family who run a hardware store out in Scarborough," mumbled one of the second sopranos during theory class one morning, the slow shake of her head revealing fully what she thought of the location.

"I heard he was a refugee from eastern Germany," added another.

"You mean ..."

"Yes. She's seeing a Jew."

"You think she even knows?"

"Hard to say. I don't imagine they see a lot of them up on the farm, if you know what I mean."

Truth be told, the gossip being hissed around the classroom had been fairly accurate. Eli had indeed been rescued from Austria as a boy in the late 1930s through the grace of a brave and active Lutheran charitable organization, and the foresight of a father who knew what fate would greet him should he stay in his homeland. And he had zigzagged his early childhood through a series of orphanages in England, before finally being adopted into a family of Scottish extraction, who soon after immigrated to east-end Toronto. The other accuracy, though actually unintended, was young Maggie's understanding of their differences. Given the homogeneous world where she had been raised, she had had no previous contact with anyone of Jewish descent (nor of any other religion of the world for that matter), and in the absence of such knowledge had fostered instead nothing but unmitigated fascination. Quite simply, she found Eli Benowitz to be a completely and utterly interesting person. By his words, his gestures ... his ideas. Especially his ideas ...

Their very first outing had proved it to her, despite the fact that it had begun as a rather one-sided disposition on Eli's part about his burgeoning love of architecture – which, she quickly learned, was the professional school he yearned to attend upon the completion of his double major bachelor's degree in mathematics and philosophy. "I have very definite ideas about architecture and I know exactly where we can go to demonstrate them," he had stated categorically not three minutes after picking her up at the front door of her dormitory, while her roommate watched from the window above, unable to imagine how Maggie Calloway, ever the centre-of-attention, would survive an afternoon with this odd little duck.

Yet survive she did, right from the outset, never once even slightly burdened by his whole-hearted dive into the pursuit that occupied him. In fact, to listen to such eager discourse, for once, on a topic other than music, was for Maggie as refreshing as the amazingly warm late-autumn day which they were sharing. And how pleasantly surprising was the confidence and enthusiasm in his voice, the awkwardness she had perceived back in the rehearsal hall now nowhere to be found as he spoke at length about his interests. Form, design, structure. It made no difference what her classmates would think, that the things of which he spoke so passionately were not common courting topics of conversation for other boys … Canadian boys. It made no difference in the least. Because he had chosen her, as much an outsider to his dreams as he was to hers. He had chosen her to talk about those dreams, to expound upon them … to be his sounding board … his audience.

The chatter centered around his love of "architectural dualities", as he had put it. Of form versus function; of space versus cavity; of the essential tensions necessary in the art of creating a structure, he said. But whereas she had envisioned a day spent strolling through the halls of Casa Loma, or perhaps down lower Church Street to be shown the details of Metropolitan United or St. Michael's, or perhaps wandering by some of the more magnificent estates along the quiet streets of Rosedale, it came to young Maggie's complete surprise when Eli ushered her across Mount Pleasant Avenue and down into a well-worn dirt footpath that led into the unmanicured undergrowth of the Don Valley. Between the brittle-brown grasses and the stands of oak and maple all but shed for the coming winter they followed a leaf-covered trail that crept and curved its way lower and lower into the ravine, taking them further and further from the bustle of downtown, the storefronts, the office buildings – further, in fact, from any architecture at all. Frequently he stopped and glanced back in the direction from which they had come, cocking his head to listen for someone or something he was not yet prepared to share. For her part Maggie followed along dutifully, watching him curiously and silently, until finally he came to one last definitive halt.

"Here," he announced, seemingly satisfied. Quickly he slipped off his jacket, flattened it down on the brown grass beside the trail, and with a flourish invited her to sit.

"So … I have a theory," he began.

"I imagine you have many," she replied, tucking her skirt under her calves as she reclined.

"True, but lately I've been aware that most of them may hinge upon this one as their foundation."

"A theory about your theories?"

"Yes. Well … maybe. I'm not entirely sure."

"Is it about architecture?"

He thought a moment. "I would say architecture is answerable to it, yes."

"Then why did you lead me out into the woods, Eli?" She felt herself smile when she said it. Felt her shoulder rise toward her chin and hoped that, in the midst of his theory-sharing, he might notice too.

"Do you have any classes over in the east wing?"

She shook her head.

"Well there's a painting in the foyer there. A landscape. One of the Group of Seven, I think. Harris maybe. At least it has his style. You see, when I was young I wanted to be a painter, and like every kid who takes it up I wanted to do landscapes. After all, when you're ten years old, mountains and rivers are more dramatic than a bowl of fruit or a portrait of your aunt. Here … I have something for you."

He pulled from his pocket what, because of their inexact folding and various sizes, could best be described as a bundle of pictures ripped, it appeared, from a number of books and magazines. "I want you to look through these."

"This is your theory?" she questioned skeptically.

"Just leaf through and tell me which you like best," he instructed.

"Why?"

"Just look at them all, and then pick out your favourite. No, better yet, three. Pick your three favourites."

Maggie slowly shuffled through the photos, all of which were depictions of countryside vistas. Some were rural and pastoral – not unlike her own home, she thought to herself. Others offered glimpses of more untamed wilderness. The Rocky Mountains. The Canadian Shield. Lake Superior. The Pacific Ocean crashing against a rugged shoreline. After two passes through the entire pile, she drew out a shot of the Chateau Lake Louise, then a picture of rolling yellow prairie beneath a thundercloud sky that was labelled 'Near Chaplin, Saskatchewan' and, finally, a photo of a small shack beside what appeared to be the St. Lawrence River. The label 'La Pocatière' had been pencilled into the bottom corner.

"Excellent!" Eli exclaimed, and fanned out the three pictures on the lining of his jacket. "Most everyone picks these or something like them."

"Most everyone? Do you bring all your dates out here for this little experiment, Eli Benowitz?" Her chin and her shoulder met again and she drew her knees up to her chest.

"Pardon? Oh no," he blushed. "I just meant my mom and dad and some aunts and uncles. Just my family ... here in Toronto."

It was at that moment she first noticed it, revealed in just the briefest pause, interrupting his enthusiasm as he tried to throw off the words *my family* so casually. It was but a flash really, yet a flash of unmistakable sadness. Despair even, blinking once and then disappearing all in the same moment.

"Everyone picks the Saskatchewan picture," he continued a split-second later. "They'll tell you it's because of the dramatic storm clouds and because they say the prairie looks so vast."

"I actually like the little farmhouse in the bottom corner."

"Exactly!" Eli almost shouted, before immediately editing his excitement. "Exactly," he repeated more calmly. "Was it the same with the little barn beside the St. Lawrence?"

Maggie nodded. "It's so small against its surroundings. In both pictures really. You sort of want to cheer for whoever lives there."

Eli jumped to his feet so fast that he had to catch his glasses from falling off the bridge of his nose. "That's it! That's my theory exactly!" he exclaimed.

"What is? I don't understand."

"Exactly what you just described. The relationship between any given structure and its surroundings. The necessary balance. You found these pictures more beautiful ... more beautiful than all the photos you did not select, which you will note were of either complete wilderness or of manmade constructs. But in your pictures the vast ruggedness that is so much of this country is balanced and juxtaposed with just a small portion of humanity. There's a proportionality – a balance, if you will. My theory is that architecture must be answerable to that sense of balance. And if I am successful in making architecture my vocation then it will be my responsibility to make sure that whatever I design and whatever I build is suitably humble against its natural setting. I have to make sure that a structure's location does not end up corrupted or compromised by my ambitions."

He stopped to stare back once more at the trail they had just ambled down, casting his gaze up through the open weave of barren branches to the few rooftops that peaked through from beyond. Her eyes followed his until suddenly she realized and jumped up beside him.

"That's what you're looking for, isn't it? " she blurted out. "A balance of these woods with just a bit of the city."

Eli nodded. "In the summer the foliage hides even more. You can just see the one rooftop. That one there." He moved behind her and pointed to the tallest of the visible gables – red brick with a tiny rounded window under its peak – and in doing so felt her leaning back against his chest.

"So you must come here a lot?"

"Whenever I need a break from the city. I like the wilderness, really. My uncle used to take me on trips up north. Up on the Bruce Peninsula."

She spun to face him, ready and eager to tell him that she knew the area well; that she had been raised just south of there on a farm overlooking Georgian Bay. But then, out of nowhere, a pair of images stopped her in her tracks. The first, of her mother, head-in-hands wondering what in heaven's name her daughter was doing down in the woods alone with a strange boy, was, of course, not unpredictable. But it was the second – the same flash of despair she had just seen unmasked on the boy's face a moment earlier – that both froze and beguiled her. She did not know what to make of it.

"Go on," she mustered.

"My uncle … well, he was my adoptive mother's brother, to be accurate. He came to Canada a few years earlier, convinced my parents they should come over too … which was fortunate. You see, Uncle Bill raised me as much as anyone. Always took an interest in what I was reading or studying. He was a real outdoorsman. He hunted and fished. Tried to teach me to do the same … without much success, I'm afraid. But I wasn't a complete fish out of water. I really liked going up there. In fact, I think it was the way he shared his love of the wilderness that's at the root of my theory."

Eli dropped to his knees with the sudden need to sift through the heap of photographs again, though, to Maggie's eye, somewhat absently. As if his mind was somewhere other than on the pictures. As if it was somewhere, unlike the date up until then, unplanned.

"There's one other thing I liked about my uncle …" he continued eventually. "But it may not be something you'll like to hear …"

She watched as he struggled further with his thoughts, then dropped the photos with a sigh, sitting back cross-legged on his jacket. She came down to meet him, her knees again drawn up to her chest, her skirt pinned down with her feet, head to the side and resting on her forearms. Her bright green eyes were fixed on him. Her gentle smile bade him go on.

"Are you religious, Maggie?"

Her head popped up. "Am I religious?"

"Yes. Are you?"

She paused, momentarily at a loss to find an adequate response, though what would eventually come out was probably the most truthful reply possible, given the limits of her small-town Ontario upbringing. ('Twelve different denominations in our little community,' her father was frequently fond of noting. 'A bit of something for anyone,' he would proudly proclaim, though in truth as far as small-town Ontario in the 1950s was concerned that *bit of something* was far less a spectrum of choice than a slight variation on one colour.)

"Am I religious?" she repeated mostly to herself as she stared off into the branches above her. "Well …"

"Yes?"

"As much as the next person, I guess," she replied with a shrug.

Eli nodded. "Well my uncle was not. And I admired him for that. Does it upset you that I would say such a thing?" She shrugged a second time, her eyes locked on him as his nervous hands sought to fondle the photos once more.

"I remember on one of our trips up north, he took me to this tiny little Anglican church they built back in the thirties. It's well up the Bruce Peninsula out in the middle of nowhere really. A little village called Cape Chin. I had been telling him that I was seriously considering studying architecture, so he thought if that was the case, I might like to see this place. And he was right. It's this beautiful bright limestone church all quarried and cut from local stone. And the interior wood milled from the groves right there near the village. Apparently people wanted something firm and permanent out there in the woods and that's what they got, thanks to determination of their local minister. Which was all fine and good except that my uncle, the outdoorsman, could never get over the words that same minister had used to ensure those buttresses were sloped just so, and lancet windows were fitted just right, and a bell tower was included. 'There's no excuse for making a house of God in the wilderness as uncouth as the wilderness itself.' It's right there in an open journal for anyone to read when they walk in the place. But to my Uncle Bill it was clearly a sign of a man at odds with his surroundings. When the same forests and woods that he loved so much were described as *uncouth* ... well, in his mind, what else might the good reverend say? Savage? Evil? In dire need of Godly cultivation and taming?

"Now I want you to know I'm not completely naïve here. I realize that the outdoors are far prettier in photographs or oil paints than when you're hiking through brambles and poison ivy patches, or when you're chopping your supply of wood with a cloud of blackflies snapping at your neck. But I also know this: For a man like my uncle, who only ever discussed God in terms of a babbling brook or mighty pine – if he did at all – it was remarks like that which turned him away from religion for good ... and right up until the day he died."

Eli paused to stretch and straighten the sagging arc that was his spine. "And I must say I would have to agree," he added a moment later. "I mean, every time my family took me to Church or to Sunday school, that's mostly what I heard. That same kind of anger. I just grew to believe it was a natural and necessary tenet of all things religious. That is, until I heard you rehearsing the *Messiah* at school."

He paused again and for the first time turned his gaze toward her as fully and intently as she was offering hers. "Look, I think you should know I'm not what you would call fluent in either my native Hebrew heritage or my adopted Presbyterianism. Who knows, maybe I am a fish out of water. All I know is when I heard you singing ..." His voice trailed away without finishing the thought.

"So your uncle died?"

"A year ago this June."

Lying in bed that night she would replay their afternoon together in her mind over and over. She would wonder why she didn't speak up, confide that the church of which he spoke was called St. Margaret's Chapel, that it was actually a mere 40 miles from her home, that she had in fact sung there as a teenager as part of an anniversary service. Perhaps the moment had simply sped by too quickly, she told herself ... sped by in favour of so much more wonderfully, deliciously, terrifying moments ... moments from which such mundane information could have only served to bring an uninvited retreat.

She flung open her dorm room window and, grabbing a spare pillow and squeezing it tightly to her body, tossed herself back upon her bed. Once more she went over the rapturous details in her mind.

The last thing she saw clearly was his sadness again; his longing lost eyes swimming in the space between them. And then suddenly he was reaching for her with an awkward urgency that she answered eagerly, lunging forward, grabbing him around his narrow ribcage, pulling him back on top of her. Their lips were clumsy as they pinched against each other, their attempts at words soon lost to the sounds of heavy gasps of unrehearsed kisses. Her hands were smooth against his back. Up and down, pulling free his shirttail with an unrealized need to feel his skin right on her, to smooth and knead the yearning ache she could feel inside him. She felt the warmth of him. On her mouth and her cheeks. Then the cool breeze below, her skirt no longer pinned. She felt free and captured all at once. She wanted to move her skin with the wind and yet be pinned frozen to his body. On they went, pressing themselves against one another with pent-up urgency neither could have professed to own, kissing and caressing whatever of the other got in the way. Time raced, then stopped, then raced on again; forever in an instant, until finally unleashing all restraint she pulled at his belt and freed him beneath the billow of her skirt. Felt him there. Pressing, panting …

~DECEMBER 11, 2010~

"*Not too quickly,*" Allison heard the elderly woman whisper, her left hand gripping the armrest as she squirmed forward on her seat, her bony right hand petting the air in front of her, guiding the mezzo through the opening passage of her aria.

> *Oh thou that tellest good tidings to Zion …*
> *… Arise, shine, for thy light has come*

"*Yes … yes,*" she cooed. "*Like that.*"

~WINTER 1951~

Eli Benowitz lived for the most part in the finished basement apartment of his parents' Scarborough home. He had made the request to move
there shortly after the death of his closest friend in the world, his Uncle Bill.
His studies were growing more and more rigorous, he claimed; his need
for quiet and privacy was increasing. And since finances, for all concerned,
precluded a move to school residence or to a downtown flat, the practical
solution, as Eli suggested, was to attack the space beyond his mother's cold
room with two-by-four wall frames, plywood, plaster, wallpaper and floor
tile.

His parents had agreed, Mrs. McLean being neither hurt nor surprised
by her son's request. He had always been one to keep to himself anyway,
locked in his bedroom most of his free time, reading, drawing, studying.
She had long since accepted that this was simply the way he was. In fact,
it was this very accepting nature that had allowed her brand of mother-
hood to succeed where all previous fostering had failed. Eli had not been
an oblivious infant, she realized, when he had been stripped from his family and severed from his roots. He had been six years old. He had seen and
lived the horror fully. So of course there was pain and anger somewhere
inside the boy's ever-neutral expression. Nightmares of loss and separation
and fear. But it was not her place to reach in and pull them out. Not at the
expense of what he needed more … his space.

"This room will be yours," she had stated gently on the first day they
took him in to their small Portsmouth flat. "Yours and yours alone. We
won't come in unless we're invited, but you can come out anytime you
want." It was a promise that she and her husband would steadfastly keep
throughout his childhood, and in a sense, a promise they further honoured
with the renovation of their basement.

It was a cramped narrow room somewhat lacking in natural light, save for that from the one ground-level window that looked out onto the front tires of his father's sedan when his parents were home, the neighbour's foundation when they were busy over at the hardware store. The low ceiling did not help, making the room seem more constrained than it actually was, and Maggie often found herself hunching unnecessarily whenever he brought her there. As for the bed, it had a most disconcerting and discernible creak which, on her first few visits at least, necessitated frequent reassurances on Eli's part that no one was ever home upstairs in the daytime … that no one would hear the slow steady crescendo of those squeaks beating out their afternoon refrain.

She found the apartment to be undeniably Eli. There were stacks of books bedside, desk-side and tableside, many left open and piled upon one another, most all of them with passages underlined, notes pencilled along the margins. Books on engineering. Books on physical science. Math books. And, of course, many, many books specifically about architecture. Treatises, tomes, reference books … biographies of people whom she assumed were famous architects. All of them waiting in the shadows, just to the side of the room's one and only light – a 40-watt desk lamp that leaned over the ink blotter on the boy's bureau. She loved its clearly defined beam, loved that the dark little cocoon that it lit was where this intellect was put through its paces, racing through and past all these books, devouring everything they had to offer. And, naturally, she loved that she was part of it. This had become their place. Their Eden brought indoors. Their own secret garden free of the world and all its protocols, stripped of expectations and clothing, until there was nothing but endless afternoons of pulsing affection honed and directed by the sweet sound of her encouragement – still awkward perhaps by the standards of more schooled lovers, yet with a growingly steady and discernible rhythm.

Even in the afterglow, the little room held its warmth. With their breath still laboured, their bodies still entwined, she would entertain him with demonstrations of her craft: proper tone, diaphragm breathing, pitch control, all the "nuts and bolts" – as he would call it – that went into the creation of the high art that was her singing. For his part, he would grab one of his weighty texts and attempt to explain some algebraic theorem or law of physics, or perhaps revisit his original theory about constructs and wilderness, which had wooed her so successfully in the first place.

And yet it wasn't until that fateful afternoon – their fifth time together there – with their torrid needs already met, their playful banter already spent, and the two of them basking in the safe warmth of the desk lamp's glow that Maggie finally answered the need to confess the whereabouts of her family home. She described at length the view of the bay from her bedroom window, the orchard that framed the yard, the roll of the fields, the view of the deep blue bay …

"And you say it's not far from where my uncle was raised?"

"Do you remember passing through a town called Wiarton?"

Eli nodded. "That's where my uncle did his shopping."

"Our farm is out the shore road from there."

"Sounds beautiful."

"You should come for a visit."

"Really?" He shot to attention, catching some of her hair as he did.

"Ouch. Yes. Maybe next summer? When classes are out. I'll ask Mother the next time she comes down."

"Not your Dad?"

"It's Mother we need to ask." She stated this matter-of-factly. "If I have good test scores from my classes and she feels like I've done well, I might be able to convince her. No doubt she will have scheduled a bunch of recitals for the Women's Institutes and the Library. But later on … June maybe?"

"But wouldn't your father–"

"Father will be haying by June. You can help him on the wagons if you like. Or with the mows in the barn. Mother won't let me. She says the dust and the heat will affect my voice."

He held up her hand, weaving his fingers in hers, raising them until the desk light glistened pink off the edge of their skin.

"What does your Dad think of your singing? I mean here you are down in the big city away from the farm. His only child. His little girl ..."

She rolled over on his chest, bringing a blanket along to keep her naked body somewhat covered. "Eli Benowitz," she said with her best tempting smile, "you do pick a most interesting moment to bring up my Daddy, don't you?"

"I was just curious," he replied, and instinctively reached for more covers himself. "It's just that I haven't heard you really talk about him very much."

"Well he's a hard person to talk about."

"Strict?"

"No. Not overly."

"What, then?"

"Well he's just a very quiet person." She put her head down flat on his chest and listened for his heartbeat. "You're right, he's probably not thrilled with the idea of me being so far away. But at least he's ... oh, what's the right word?"

"Proud?"

"No. Well perhaps, but he would keep that bit of news to himself. No, I was going to say that when it comes to my singing he's ... well, affected."

"Affected?"

"Oh that sounds strange, doesn't it? What I mean is ... well, what do I mean? OK, let's just say this. I'm sure people who know my folks, or at least think they do, believe that Mother rules the roost and my father does whatever he's told. Especially when it comes to me."

"But that's not true?"

"Only to a point. I mean Mother is the one who has always tried to further my musical studies, not my father. But at least with him, whenever I sing somewhere and he's in the audience ... even though he doesn't gush over me like Mother, I always know he's listening. I mean really listening. I guess that's what I'm trying to say. He likes it when I sing. He's not worried whether someday I'll become some famous professional singer. He just likes to hear me sing."

She rolled over on her back, keeping her head propped on Eli's ribcage. "I used to like helping him in the barn … feeding the calves, spreading out the straw bedding for them. Just him and me. Even after Mother made her 'no barn' rule, I still found a way to sneak out. Usually I'd put one of her opera records on the phonograph in the upstairs hall and she'd quite proudly assume I was upstairs in my room furthering my music education. I'd always end up in the old silo. It wasn't being used even back then … not since a storm took most of the roof back in '32. But it was just the best place to sing. I loved the way my voice resonated inside. And on the nights when the moon would shine through, it was really quite magical. I'll show you when you come to visit."

"I'd like that."

"I remember the very first time I went in there," she continued with a giggle. "I was only four or five years old. There was this old ladder that ran up the inside wall and I guess it was in pretty poor shape. But I was an adventurous little thing, so up I went. I'd climb a few rungs and then sing, and then climb a few more and sing again. Anyway, by the time my father found me I was most of the way up, swinging from the ladder, leaning back and swaying with one hand holding on and the other waving in the air. I must have scared him because he climbed up there so fast and hauled me down, all the time saying, 'NEVER AGAIN … NEVER AGAIN …' It was the only time I ever remember him yelling at me … this big scolding voice filling up the silo, way more than mine had …'What were you doing up there?' And of course I answered quite happily that I was singing to the moon, which must have seemed like a very silly reason for such a dangerous stunt because he started lecturing me all over again. Did I know how old and weak those rungs were? Did I know that the wood is nearly split on several of them? And, of course, then I saw how much he was shaking, and so I started crying and carrying on."

She lifted herself up on an elbow and played with the hairs of his chest. "He tucked me in that night. He usually left that to Mother, but that time he came in to make sure I was OK. I was still sobbing a little, but when I saw he wasn't angry anymore, I worked up enough nerve to ask him if I could still go into the silo to sing if I promised to never, never, ever climb up the ladder, ever again. I can remember how he touched my forehead and told me that would be OK. 'In fact me and the cows just might like that,' he said …"

Her voice trailed away, for a moment lost in her childhood, until Eli rolled her onto her back. "Thank you for that," he whispered in her ear. Following a deep and long kiss, he rose up and, with newfound confidence, renewed their lovemaking once more.

•

… so what you're saying is that people subconsciously want a balance between their homes and the land around them?

– *I'm saying there has to be a balance between a structure and its surroundings, yes.*

And this relates to Emerson Place how?

– *Were you listening at all? Obviously it's a translation of the very same theory. Only in this case, we don't consider the external size of the structure against its backdrop, but the quality of the inner space that surrounds the music!*

I'm sorry, but I'm not sure I follow the connection–

– *Oh of course not. Christ, why should you be any different?*

Now Eli, please be fair–

*– Fair? Fair, she says. OK tell me this. Suppose
people do come away from Emerson Place all
tickled and thrilled with the concert they've just
heard. Tell me, who are they going to credit, huh?
Take a guess!*

Well … everyone, I suppose.

– More specific than that. Who?

Well the soloists. The conductor. The orchestra and
the choir.

*– Right. And you know what? They'd still be
missing the entire goddamn point. I mean way off!
Christ, and she tells me to be fair.*

I'm sorry, Eli. I'm trying to understand what you're–

*– NOBODY. Not the audience. Not the musicians.
Hell, not even the bloody soloist herself will take
the time to pay tribute to the actual room. And
No, I'm not talking about the bloody columns, or
the facade, or the stage or the seats … Hell, they'll
all get their share of heavy petting. I'm talking
about the cavity. I'm talking about the space in
between all of that. The space where the music
either breathes or suffocates. The space that takes
the breath of voice drawn from the throat and
articulated through the lips and tongue; takes
those pleasing waves of sound and preserves them,
sustains them. But when she's completed her last
note and she's taking her deep grand bows and
getting all that applause, do you think she'll be any
closer to finally realizing any of this?*

Realizing any of what, Eli? I'm sorry, but it just feels
like we're dancing around in circles without ever really getting around to what you really want to say–

*– I'm talking about her muse. Her muse, goddamn
it! I'm talking about the realization that it's not
some conductor, or some voice coach or George
fucking Handel himself. It's the one who creates*

*that space! That's what I'm goddamn talking
about! (click)*

•

Wind whistles around barren tree limbs above him. The meadow has now given way to forest, first scrubby saplings – the remnant of an old overcut woodlot – then deeper into the inky darkness of untamed undulating landscape.

He considers the concert once more and, with the accuracy that all his previous treks have afforded, gauges where they would be by now. Much like the meadow back behind his shoulder, the Pastoral Sinfony would now be over. Next would be the nativity cycle – Handel's take on Shepherds … and Angels. Good Tidings. Great Joy.

The wind whistles louder. Colder. The tree limbs creak and groan under the strain. It's all he can do to endure this part of the journey. All he can do to go on.

~MARCH 1951~

Concern came first from her voice teacher, arriving in the form of a letter addressed to Maggie's parents.

Dear Mrs. Calloway,

Please find enclosed a copy of Maggie's mid-term grades for both music performance and her elective classes. During our initial meetings and in the many subsequent visits to my office

you have continually expressed the desire to see your daughter pursue her singing as a career. Unfortunately, as you will note from these transcripts, her scores, while more than adequate for graduation in a few years, are quite frankly far below the standards of someone with such lofty aspirations. Since the opportunities for professional vocal work are quite confined, competition for such work is extremely strong. It is therefore in your best interest to heed my concerns. Maggie's work has been suffering and her results declining over the past two semesters. So much so that it is my belief that the time has come to intervene.

I still do believe that your daughter has been blessed with a singular and exquisite talent. But if we are to see this talent through to the heights it deserves, then we first need to implement a strategy by which she will be both motivated and dedicated in her training. Without such a plan, I fear my role as your daughter's voice instructor here at the college and, indeed, her pursuit as a professional soloist are both destined to be fruitless endeavours.

Please respond with an appropriate time that we could meet to discuss the matter in more detail.

With regards,

Prof. Enid Blaisdell
Dept. of Music
St. Timothy's College

■

Mrs. Calloway and her husband arrived at 9:00 a.m. the next morning.

Dr. Blaisdell had expected no less, having begun preparations for their arrival even before their telegram promising her they would be right down had been delivered to her office. (A telegram she had read with a rare smirk, as she rather cynically wondered whether a similar meeting would be scheduled with Maggie's Canadian Literature professor, who had in fact given their daughter a far more distressing mark than she had received in any of her music classes.)

The first portion of the preparation had been her call to an old colleague – the esteemed Florence Matthias, founder and headmistress of England's renowned Lincoln Voice Academy – who just happened to be visiting as a guest lecturer the same week that Blaisdell chose to inform the Calloways of their daughter's struggles. The second part had been to schedule Miss Matthias in her office immediately before she *made time* to step out and greet the Calloways, and to ask her secretary to fetch Maggie from her Music History Class.

Blaisdell began the meeting with a lecture of considerable length before she even so much as acknowledged, let alone introduced, her guest. Maggie simply had to focus more steadfastly on her training. She had to score far more favourably on her semester's test pieces, the next round of which would be adjudicated at the end of term. There was no more room for mediocrity, she warned. No more room for laziness and excuses. A beautiful voice – even one as beautiful as hers – was of no artistic worth whatsoever if it could not refine, control and produce its beauty when called upon to do so. Favourable test results were therefore a must, she reiterated. Favourable results would mean Maggie's future might indeed still be bright. Favourable results – and here Blaisdell finally gestured towards the imposingly silent woman in the corner – might even be reason for a recommendation of provisional admittance into Miss Matthias' private academy to complete her degree in Music Performance. But this could only come to pass, the professor was quick to add, if the girl's very real potential was realized over the balance of the current school term.

The details were then spelled out. The financial burden of enrolling abroad, it was explained, would be offset primarily by a bursary offered to foreign students at the academy, but also eased with occasional solo work in the Lincoln Cathedral. Furthermore, Maggie could take on young voice students herself in the evenings, if additional income was required and her own training schedule permitted. Lodging would be at a rooming house owned by the academy, austere but reasonable and offering no distractions. Suitable for young women like Maggie, Blaisdell explained.

There was a pause of disbelief as mother and daughter stared at one another and then gazed alternately between the severe expressions of the two women before them, the juxtaposition of their grimly-set jaws momentarily clouding the realization of the opportunity they had just presented. And then like an explosion, the room was suddenly alive with uncontrollable excitement, both Maggie and her mother jumping to their feet, grabbing each other by the arms, squealing and spinning in circles until Mrs. Calloway thought to break free to lunge across the desk and grab Dr. Blaisdell's hands, lauding her for the faith and interest she had shown in her daughter.

"This is not my doing," the professor responded soberly, and with a not-quite-under-her-breath *all right then …all right*, struggled to free one of her own hands from the woman's grip and motion to the corner chair.

Maggie bounced over to the woman immediately, knocking over a wastebasket and a jar of pens in the process. "Yes … Thank you, Mrs. Matthias," she gushed. "Thank you so incredibly much!"

"It's Miss."

"Miss … right. Thank you. And don't worry. I'm not going to let anything spoil this opportunity … this unbelievably generous opportunity. Mother, did you hear? I'm going to sing in an English Cathedral … oh Mother, you must come over too!"

"Young Lady, please know we shall not waver on even one of the conditions of this offer. I rarely take on students without first-hand knowledge of their talents, but Enid is a dear and respected colleague and she has convinced me that your talent alone warrants consideration."

"Oh yes ... thank you too, Dr. Blaisdell," the girl blurted out, and doubled back to submit the poor professor to another round of clumsily exuberant hand-shaking.

"But talent alone ..." the English woman cut in, cooling the room with her tone, "... talent alone without dedication is a waste of both time and finances." She glanced over the top of her spectacles towards the girl's parents and elicited an alliance of cautionary nods from both.

"We understand completely, don't we, Maggie?" Mrs. Calloway replied

"And you will work hard from here on in," Blaisdell added. It was a statement, not a question.

"Oh yes, Dr. Blaisdell, harder than ever," Maggie gushed, and danced another giggling jig with her mother until she gasped for breath. "Oh my goodness ... I just can't believe this day! I just can't. Oh my, I think I have to sit down." She flung herself back into her chair, holding her stomach from the excitement that had just energized her life.

"I'm sorry," she panted. "I'm just a little bit—"

"Still feeling a bit under the weather?" the professor asked quietly.

"It's my stomach again."

"It's just the excitement, Dear," her mother beamed.

"Yes, perhaps," Blaisdell responded. "But to be on the safe side, why not rest outside my office in one of the armchairs. You can use the faculty washroom if you get feeling nauseous. I have a few more things to discuss with your parents."

With one final volley of gratitude, Maggie rose again and dismissed herself, then skipped gleefully for the hall, her euphoria rebounding to preclude her from noticing the cramping in her abdomen any further – so slight, after all, was its twinge compared to this unbelievable turn of events. But that would not be the only detail to elude the young music major that morning. Not in the least. For in her giddiness she would also fail to notice how quickly the door had closed directly behind her. Fail to hear the sombre click of the lock that followed. Fail to catch the voice of Florence Matthias, slipping out from under the jamb just before that lock could seal in the conversation she left behind. "*Now ... to discuss the source of this girl's distractions. Enid, you mentioned this Jewish boy ...*" Failed completely to appreciate the subdued expressions on her parents' faces – their look now far more aligned with that of the professor – when they finally emerged from behind that locked door an hour later ...

"Come with us, Maggie," her mother spoke. "We've been kindly invited to a dinner tonight hosted by Miss Matthias. Tomorrow we see a doctor about that stomach of yours."

Aria:
He was despised …

The Oratorio: A Brief Introduction

Perhaps the rise of the oratorio as a popular 18th-century musical form can best be described as a stylistic response to issues confronting composers of the day. First and foremost, it was a practical alternative to the ever larger, ever grander, but ever more cumbersome full opera productions which had come to burden London's musical societies both logistically and financially. In the oratorio such companies found a more manageable production; in effect an unstaged dramatic singing of a narrative or text.

But with their often religious themes, oratorios also served to bridge the perpetually tenuous gap that existed between the Church and Music Societies of that era. And though Handel would have undoubtedly flown his flag first and foremost in the latter's camp, it is clear the popularity of his oratorios owed a great debt to traditions that preceded him in the life of the Church itself. The religious ode, for example, was a scripturally themed song or poem presented for a congregational audience – albeit often only grudgingly by the Church hierarchy – during the celebration of St. Cecilia, patron saint of music. And one can see its influence, if not as a direct precursor for Handel himself, then at least for the appetites of those who attended and revelled in his concerts.

Yet the tension inherent in this alignment of musical and religious interest cannot be overstated, for whereas performances of Handel's *Messiah* now regularly grace sanctuaries and cathedrals, at the outset the Church frowned upon any work that "tinkered with the sanctity of scripture". This strain most likely came to a head when Handel attempted to secure the services of the best singers and musicians available for his inaugural performance of *Messiah* in 1742, as most of Dublin's talent was already in the employ of the Church and they were deemed off-limits to sing in a company of fiddlers, as the Dean of St. Patrick's Cathedral had referred to the production.

"So what have we learned?" Peter chimed as he plopped back into his chair with two more pints in tow.

"The origins of the oratorio."

"Really?" Peter grabbed the book unceremoniously from his friend's hands. "Do they contrast it from the *opera seria*?" He asked eagerly, skimming over the paragraph Kyle had just finished reading. "Well ... barely," he sighed, and slapped the book back on the table. "Very well. Here's the deal."

"Should I settle in?"

"You should. You see, Handel was a major part of the London music scene before he took off for Ireland to write *Messiah*. Hell, he basically introduced that city to opera. And sure, Florence and Milan would tell a different tale, but the fact is Italian composers were just as apt to be selling their works to London audiences as back home. And by the mid-1700s, we are talking the high season where everybody was writing bigger, more dramatic epics, with longer and longer scores, massive casts and set designs. I mean, the opera houses of Paris even had stables down under their stages just to keep horses or cattle or whatever might be needed for a particular production. And Handel himself wrote an opera where they let loose a flock of sparrows in the hall each and every night."

"Poor janitor."

"Yes, well the point is ... it was all just getting to be too much."

"So along came the oratorio."

"Along came the oratorio. No sets. No props. No costumes ..."

"No livestock."

"You two wanted a couple of Smithwick's?" the waiter interrupted.

"Simon, my friend. It's been so long ..." Peter replied, spinning around in his chair.

"Sorry for the wait, Gents. The good weather has packed the place ... caught us a bit short-staffed I'm afraid."

"No worries, we understand completely. Unfortunately our thirst was far less patient. We ended up going to the bar ourselves. Sorry."

"Ah but what the hell, right?" Kyle piped up cheerfully, plucking the glasses happily from the serving tray.

"Kyle!"

"What?" his friend countered with a shrug and a glance at his watch. "Waste not, want not. Besides, Simon came all this way and we still have a good hour."

"I'll start a tab," the waiter monotoned and headed on to his next table.

"Thank you, Simon," Peter called back over his shoulder. "Now, where were we?"

Kyle pressed his index finger to the open page on the table. "The history of the oratorio, and odes and something about a St. Cecilia's Day," he replied in his best attempt at an English accent.

"November 16th as I recall. She was a defender of the arts."

"So I read. Apparently classical music wasn't really appreciated by the Church back then."

"Can we relate?" Peter raised his glass. "Although I still say you should come with me to Redeemer up on Bloor some Sunday. They've got a great choir. A lot of the guys in my choral class sing up there. And the priest there is really positive; very liberal ... actually has come to terms with the fact it's now 1982."

Kyle shrugged, but said nothing in response, his eyes having fallen on a young couple sauntering along the sidewalk, their eyes locked on one another, safely oblivious to everyone else around them.

"The church back in Handel's day, on the other hand," Peter continued, "... not so forward thinking. In fact they were extremely wary of anybody playing around with what they considered to be the absolute Word of God ... Oh crap!"

"Still pissed at them are we?"

"No. I just remembered I have to feed a meter," Peter replied, jumping suddenly from his chair.

"Oh that's right. Mr. Blue Skies drove."

"Yeah, yeah, yeah ... here, have some more quality time with the program," he called back, and tossed the syllabus over the heads of two tables of customers, straight into his date's lap. "Look up tonight's soloists."

"Come back when you can stay awhile."

"Yeah, yeah ..."

~1987~

"So what has that granddaughter of yours decided?" she called out loudly, having strode into the Bluewater Tavern as though it were her local of twenty years. She plopped herself down beside him, waving to the barkeeper with a self-importance that communicated in no uncertain terms that he'd better get out from behind his counter if he wanted her business. Murray glanced up, then returned his gaze to the head on his pint of ale. If he had been surprised by her entrance, he did not show it.

"She'll do the lessons," he nodded.

"Because you should know I'm going to be tough. It's the only way I know. You don't take a beautiful voice like hers and forgive away all the bad habits just in the interest of sparing some feelings."

"She'll be fine."

"Well as long as we're clear on this point right from the start. She was in an awful state after her school concert and I'd rather avoid having to console her every time she–"

"Like I said …" he interjected a little more loudly, then took a long slow sip, "she'll do just fine."

"Well as long as we're clear–"

"Ms. Calloway, with all due respect, the girl's mother died and her father walked out on her all in the span of two weeks. Given all she's been through, exactly how tough do you really think your little singing lessons are gonna be for my granddaughter?"

In most other instances, even in her retirement, such a retort would have raised a combativeness in the woman, an ire born from a career where the needs and opinions of Margaret Calloway had been routinely patronized without question – deference on her part having been an option abandoned many years before, replaced instead by a quiet but effective belligerence that worked its purpose in making promoters, musicians, even other soloists simultaneously reverent and leery of her. But this man's calm, his undeterred gaze, first down into his drink and then up to the country band assembling for their matinee set, for some reason bade her retreat from pressing the matter too much further.

"Well as long as we're clear," she repeated again – mostly for last-word's sake – then waved once more at the barkeeper, calling out curtly for a Jameson neat before leaning back in her chair, sighing and casting a long critical look around the establishment, taking in the dim surroundings of the rough grey barnboard wall treatment and the only-slightly-less grey windows, their foggy tinted panes seemingly a deliberate design to keep the light of day filtered down to a dull haze. There was tired old red carpet beneath her feet holding up what she imagined must be standard-issue bar tables, generously adorned with standard-issue ashtrays and beer-label coasters, surrounded by standard-issue spindle-back chairs. She considered the band, busily cramming their instruments and amplifiers onto their tiny stage in the far corner, near the hallway to the restrooms. Then the two heavy-set men at the bar – truck drivers, she surmised for no particular reason. There was an older man to their left, lurched over a shot glass, leaning forward and resting his forearms on a walker. And then finally, the man sitting next to her, situated – as she would come to learn – exactly where he always was on a Saturday afternoon. Alone in the centre row of tables, second from the front, arms folded, eyes off into space.

"So ..." she sighed again. "Come here often?"

Murray took another sip and then pushed the glass away from his hands and leaned back in his chair, his legs out straight in front of him. "This is my kind of music," he responded finally, with a satisfied nod towards the stage. "Was for my wife, too. A buddy of mine down at the arena, that's his son's combo up there. They play out a fair bit ... wedding receptions and the like. Those lads were good enough to play at Helen's funeral. Song called *Broken Angels.*"

"I heard that your wife passed away," she replied with a strangely absent tone as she gave the room a second less-than-accepting go-over.

"Don't worry, " he sighed. "I don't expect you to get my taste in music. I may be just simple folk, but I'm not so much of a hick that I can't see the difference between what these lads do and the style of music you're used to."

For a moment her mind was thrown back to one of the concert stages, she wasn't sure which one – the *Lyceum* in Chicago perhaps, or was it the Opera House in Houston? – and then to the vast chasm that existed between the society-page patrons of that world and the place she found herself now. She looked about her a third time, this time more out of discomfort than disapproval.

"My granddaughter's been listening to that recording you gave her. Just about every night, I'd say."

"That's good," Maggie replied still somewhat absently, as she wiped a layer of dust from the chair in front of her.

"What's it called again?"

"Handel's *Messiah*."

"And that's really you singing eh?"

Maggie nodded.

"Haven't got around to listening myself yet."

"Is that so?"

"Read the write-up on the album cover though. That was pretty interesting stuff. Went through your whole career stem to stern without missing a step."

She looked at him suspiciously. "That, I seriously doubt, Mr. Page," she replied.

"Here's your Jameson, Ma'am."

"Hmm? Oh, thank you. Do I pay you now?"

"Oh let's have Murray put this one on his tab," the barkeep replied with a wink and returned to his station to wipe down the copper surface of a counter that clearly was already well-polished. Maggie and Murray both watched him go.

"You make friends quick," the arena manager grunted.

"Oh yes, the men love me," she said with a wave of the hand as she sipped her drink.

"Write-up called you the toast of the town when it came to singing those particular songs. Said you performed just about anywhere that's anywhere. London. New York ... all over Europe."

"Well these things usually favour the highlights, don't they? Much more impressive-sounding than Fredericton, Little Rock and Huddersfield. Wouldn't you agree?"

"But it got me thinking ... that record can't be all that old 'cause it mentions your retirement down in Toronto, which was only a few years back."

"You are correct, Mr. Page. The album is a newer release. The recording, however, is not," she explained, with another trip to the rim of her glass.

"Yeah, I read that part too. Said you actually recorded those particular concerts way back in your twenties. Somewhere in England."

"Lincolnshire."

"Said they took those old tapes and did something ... *re-pressed* it?"

"Remastered."

"Yeah, that's it. *Remastered.* Oh what the hey. Wayne, maybe I will have one more today," he called over his shoulder toward the bar. "Oh, but there was one thing that did get me wondering ..."

Maggie raised her eyes up over her drink.

"Now forgive me if I'm being too nosy here but, Ma'am, for somebody who has gotten so famous singing something called the *Messiah*, you don't look like what I think of as a religious person."

The comment had a strange familiarity that both intrigued the woman and caused her to bristle, though it was the latter that won the race to her initial reply. "And why is that, exactly, Mr. Page?" she challenged. "Is my drink not temperate enough for you? Perhaps I should be sipping tea? Knitting some mittens for a Church bazaar?"

"No, Ma'am, not at all. What somebody does or drinks is completely their own business. What I'm talking about is the music itself. This *Messiah*. It's all from the Bible isn't it?"

Maggie put her drink down and stared at the man.

"Ah Geez," he winced, "now you're looking at me like 'what's this guy's point', and Lord help me, Ma'am, I'm not sure I have one. I mean the only religious music Helen and I ever listened to were a few old Johnny Cash gospel tapes she picked up on a shopping trip down to Branson a few years back. But your stuff is nothing like that."

"Really? Do you think so?" She cooed.

"I mean, the songs we'd listen to, you could sing along with them and you could remember them. I mean the tune would be right there in your head. But yours. Well, I hear Allison playing that record all the time, but for the life of me, even though it's always repeating the words over and over, well I couldn't begin to whistle you one single tune out of the lot of it."

"Best not try," she replied with a pat of his hand.

"But here's the thing I don't get," he ploughed on unaware. "All those exercises you give Allison … you know, about breathing right and hitting her notes clearly and pronouncing her words correctly. Well I know I probably have the biggest tin ear this side of Orangeville, but I'm no fool. I know Johnny and June never came close to making the grade on any of that. Not the way they like to dig in on the *r*'s and give it a bit of the nasal—"

"Mr. Page, if I could interrupt. Could you tell me if you are remotely close to making your point? Because if not, I think you would do well to order me another of these most workmanlike Irish whiskeys."

"What? Oh sure. Wayne?" He glanced over at the barkeeper, whose amused expression had not yet left the unlikely pair. "Anyway I guess what I'm asking is whether you think ole Johnny Cash is any further from heaven for not knowing how to sing properly … I mean, when you've done so much training to make sure all your singing is so perfect?"

Maggie squinted at the man, confused not only by his ramblings themselves, but by the fact that she, at least to some degree, was following them.

"Ah, I'm sorry," Murray relented. "I just get thinking 'bout stuff like this lately."

"How long were you married, Mr. Page?"

"Thirty-seven years," he sighed. "But I guess it's still what I hang my hat on. My life with her. I imagine with you it must be your singing career."

"I imagine it must be," she repeated quietly.

"I take it you never married?"

"Briefly. Back in England. A man named Russell Cochrane."

"Was he a singer too?"

"Russell? Heavens no. A patron, to be sure. But not musically inclined himself. No, he was the son of an economics professor from Cambridge University. We were set up very enthusiastically by my voice teacher during my final year of studies."

"I'm sorry. I just assumed you were so busy with your career you never–"

"Let's just say my marriage was nothing noteworthy enough to find its way onto the liner notes of a record album," she said with a slight toast, raising her drink to let the fume of it linger below her nose a moment before she continued. "Look, I was young and Russell came along at the right time with all his wealth and family connections to people of influence. It made for what seemed a very good match. Just a bit of a shame we were never actually in love ..."

"You married somebody you didn't love?"

"Yes, Mr. Page. I married somebody I didn't love," she shot back. "Go ahead. Say what you want, but the concert stage was like a drug. And as a young woman I was caught up in the power of that drug. I would sing.

Russell would smile that smile of his and then introduce me to his family connections. Pretty soon those connections were donating to concert societies and underwriting tours and recordings. Once the inertia of that process got underway, it had a momentum all its own. And that's how the 30-year career of the great Margaret Calloway was born, Mr. Page." She went ahead and drained the glass – still hovering before her – in one decisive swallow. "The marriage, on the other hand – well, it didn't make it past three."

Her eyes drifted about the room once more while Murray coughed and cleared his throat, shifting back and forth in his chair as he vainly searched for a more comfortable avenue of small talk.

"So no kids, I take it."

"We had a daughter," she returned, studying the man's uneasiness and taking stock of her own. "Christine lives in Waterloo with her husband."

"Waterloo's a nice town," he mumbled weakly. "Grandchildren?"

"Oh I think that's enough about me for one afternoon, Mr. Page," she cut in, rising and grabbing her second drink right from the bartender's tray and downing it as well, in one effortless swig. "I trust the previous Tuesday and Thursday arrangement is satisfactory for Allison's lessons?" she asked. "At 4:30, out at the house?"

Murray nodded blankly.

"Very well. I must be off. I will leave you to the particular joys of your country music." And with that she marched for the bright sliver of sunlight that had dared creep under the tavern door, pausing only to pursue one last brief thought.

"By the way?" she asked. "Did I ever *thank* you for rescuing my hat?"

Murray shook his head.

"Well …" she paused, "that was an oversight." A brief shower of sunshine splashed across the dull grey wall then the door fell shut once more.

~MARCH 1951~

Warwick Hall had been decked out most splendidly. Lace-trimmed linens underlay the finest of bone china, delicate crystal and silverware sparkled in the soft fluttering candlelight from the rows of long pewter tapers, and all of it spread out impressively along the two long guest tables which sported, at regular intervals, platters of Miss Matthias' choice of roast, deep bowls of vegetables, boatloads of gravy, steamed greens, baskets of freshly baked scones and trays of preserves and relishes. Eli's first thought, however, was not of any of these details, nor of the table setting as a whole, but instead, as was his wont, of the hall itself. He could not help feeling the event looked far too small for the size of the room chosen to host it, what with seating put out for no more than thirty people, including the small head table situated at a considerable distance along the far wall. It was a layout that, despite its smallness, suggested to the boy neither comfort nor intimacy, but rather exclusivity and privilege.

With his left shoulder still hugging the outside of the door frame he scanned the room of its mingling guests, locating first Mr. and Mrs. Calloway, whom he recognized instantly from photos Maggie had shown him. Then the significant torso of Dr. Blaisdell, whom he remembered from the *Messiah* rehearsals. He noted Maggie's roommate Betty Pierce, and a few of her fellow music students, and reasoned quite correctly that the esteemed Florence Matthias was the woman dressed in the crisp navy suit and skirt set, cradling a cup of tea as she effortlessly held court over a cluster of faculty.

"You're here!" Maggie squealed, popping out of a group of sopranos all huddled in giddy conversation, her voice echoing across the enormous room as she ran over, grabbed him by the wrists and skipped him out into the midst of the festivities.

■

The fact that Miss Matthias' dinner party had preceded Maggie's doctor appointment by twelve hours was perhaps the most important bit of chronology in the entire life of Eli Benowitz. Had it not; had the suspicions of Dr. Blaisdell and the Calloways already been confirmed medically, Eli's presence there that night would surely have never come to pass. Even as things stood, it had taken a great deal of urging on Maggie's part to convince him he would be a welcome addition to the party in the first place.

"Maggie, slow down," he had pleaded upon picking up the telephone and being bombarded by the onslaught of high-pitched glee. He couldn't keep up with her babbling. Couldn't make out the words. What was she on about? Unbelievable news? Something about a chance of a lifetime? He definitely heard the phrase 'going to school in England'. Studying at a Voice Academy. Then something else about a party. A dinner?

"Let me get this all straight," he cut in finally with a terseness that temporarily at least bid her slow down just a bit, if only to reassure him, to explain. "You want me to go to a dinner to celebrate the fact you're suddenly going to leave me?"

"It's not like that!"

"Are you serious?"

"It's just to study for a term. Three months. Four at the most. We'll be just fine. Please just be happy for me, Eli. This is such grand news."

"And did you say Warwick Hall?"

"What's wrong with Warwick?"

"It's not exactly my cup of tea, Maggie. I mean, what do I wear?"

"Oh Eli. Please don't get this way. Not tonight. Just wear your brown sports jacket. Besides, you can meet Miss Matthias. I'm sure she'll be able to tell us where you could stay if you visited. And just think of the architecture you could take in … the churches and the castles!"

"So you would still want me to visit?"

"Oh Eli …"

Perhaps had she been able to see his face … the lost sunken eyes, that once passing flash of sadness she had noticed back on their very first date, now magnified and frozen in despair. If she could have taken in that expression, perhaps she would have done better. But such had not been the case, and in the few hours between her phone call and his arrival at her party Eli had already begun to spin in the isolation of his own thoughts, slipping to that dark place where he harboured his worst fears and doubts, tenuously tethered down in his depths lest they break free and surface amidst his daily life. It was a place he had known since he was young, though not one he ever chose to explore. Nor was it a place he ever chose to share. Not with his parents, nor with Maggie – not even with Uncle Bill, the one man with whom he had shared more than anyone else. And perhaps in the end it was this fear of sharing; this fearful consequence of the darkness, rather than the darkness itself, that was Eli's undoing. Perhaps it was the *being left alone* more than loneliness itself that had created such dread. The dread he had always known was there, no matter how hard he tried to lock it up and store it away. Smother it of air and breath and light … vague memories of a woman's arms being pulled from him, as he is pushed onto a train … of standing alone on that crowded pier in Portsmouth waiting for someone … anyone … to recognize his predicament. Of awakening to the sobbing form of his father slouched at the foot of his bed, informing him how a car accident had taken his uncle. And now this … the sudden news of her imminent departure – news she chose to deliver with the same eagerness and excitement that had hitherto been reserved for him. Even as he had hung up the receiver and proceeded with the tasks of complying with her wish – brushing off his sportcoat, pressing his best trousers; washing, shaving, combing, doing all he could to bring his outwardly gangly appearance up to the standard of a Warwick Hall function – the darkness had already begun its irresistible work. She would fall in love with her new English home. She would meet more interesting people. More like-minded people. Those who better knew and appreciated her talents and her training. Other singers. Other soloists. Other men. The realizations hit him with a distinct and tangible pain ... the distant yet unmistakable muscle memory of abandonment.

That he loved her he was certain. He had told her on many occasions and she had always responded in kind, her replies more beautiful to him than the music she made. But was *love* now too strong a word? Was *love* not now too compromised to hold onto? What was their relationship now ... their time as a couple ... their now unnamed association? Mere affection? No, *affection* was an act, it wasn't a statement. It wasn't a *definition*. And a *definition* was the solid footing that he suddenly needed and craved. Clearly she was too caught up in her opportunity to consider the consequences. She was leaving, plain and simple. And though her words and actions had leapt to keep him included, as she now dragged him and the clomp of his father's hand-me-down shoes into the middle of the banquet hall – stroking his hand, nudging him shoulder to shoulder, smiling up occasionally in between the good wishes of colleagues and accolades of peers – he could not shake the inevitable notion. He was, *by definition*, an adversary of the night's celebrations, an impediment to the dreams and goals of the beautiful and talented Maggie Calloway.

That he loved her he was certain. That he *needed* her, however, was another matter, for his *need* behaved far differently. *Need* suddenly did not trust the way she lit up the room, nor the way she flitted about from classmate to classmate. *Need* resented the moments that such behaviour took her away. *Need*, in fact, had started keeping track of these moments, measuring them against those she still reserved for him. *Need* had started a tally; *need* was keeping score.

■

"Come on, my parents are here!" she bubbled, suddenly veering away from the group of students she had been talking to, pulling his arm in the opposite direction instead. The boy's free hand desperately tried to smooth out an uncooperative crease on the lapel of his jacket as she towed him along.

"Hello, Mr. Calloway. I'm Eli Benowitz," he announced with as much confidence as he could muster. "It's wonderful to finally meet you, Sir. Maggie has told me so much about her home."

There was but a momentary pause, brief yet sufficient to communicate an air of undeniable disapproval. "Bud Calloway," came the eventual hoarse reply, followed by more silence.

"Mama?" Maggie urged.

"Hello, Eli. I'm Anabeth Calloway. Margaret's mother."

"Yes, Ma'am. Like I said, it is great to finally have a chance to meet–"

"I'm sorry. Where exactly did you say you met my daughter?"

"Ma'am?"

"Oh … please excuse my curiosity. It just seems that you have us at a bit of a disadvantage. You say Maggie has talked a great deal about our home, but I'm afraid she has neglected to mention anything about you to us whatsoever."

"Mother!" Maggie scolded in a whisper.

"Well, Dear, I don't recall seeing Eli at any of your performances."

"I like to go to the rehearsals," the boy offered haplessly.

"So you're in the music program as well?"

"Mother, I told you. Eli's studying to become an architect."

"Did you, Dear?"

"Come from a big family, Eli?" Maggie's father suddenly spoke up and like a bug to a light bulb Eli eagerly headed for his words with the standard rendering of his life story, altered only by an inexplicable detour to mention how his adopted family had decided to keep the surname of his birth for him, though he knew next to nothing of his ancestry … and, of course, that his favourite uncle had often taken him camping on the Bruce Peninsula when he was younger … such beautiful country up their way, he made sure to add.

"And what did you say your last name was again?" Mr. Calloway cut him off with a quiver in his voice and a glare aimed safely toward a neutral corner of the hall. But before Eli could reply, the imposing accent of Florence Matthias announced, with a tap of her stemware, that the pork was ready for carving and requested that everyone please take their seats.

Darkness encroached again during the meal, creeping like a night tide on an unsuspecting shoreline. With conversation proving intermittent at best Eli soon chose to abandon any further attempts at socializing once it became clear that Maggie's parents, sitting with their shoulders so deliberately turned away from him, had no interest in developing any. On its own, he could have managed their silence. Could have dealt with their obvious disapproval. So, too, could he have handled the fight that would have been required to overcome such disapproval, a fight that Eli, despite his youth, already knew too well. "*Benowitz, you say. Sounds like a Jewish name,*" undoubtedly being the next line of the conversation that Maggie's father had begun had he not been interrupted. Yes, disapproval he could have worked with. Disapproval he could have managed. But neglect. Neglect was not so easy. And each time he glanced across to the head table Maggie seemed deeper and deeper in captivated conversation with Miss Matthias, a look of utter awe spread fully across her face – the look that he had so stupidly assumed had been reserved only for him and his musings. But should he really be surprised, the darkness wondered. Had her responses not been slipping of late? Just a bit? Had they not argued a few times recently; she just slightly tired of his retiring nature? Why was he there anyway? Why had she insisted he come to cheer on their imminent estrangement? To listen in on every conversation with faculty and student about how finally she would be able to realize all that potential, how nothing was going to distract her from working towards her goal? Was she actually this insensitive? Or perhaps, the darkness pressed, his presence there was actually a subconscious ambush on her part. An opportunity to sever their *affection*. A convenient means to free herself from the growing burden that was Eli Benowitz.

"No!" he almost shouted out audibly, his powers of reason straining valiantly to pull him free of the swelling wave of doubt, yank him back into the lifeboat of the here and now. It just couldn't be so! If his inclusion in the evening's festivities was actually sponsored by such a manipulative purpose – perhaps by her parents, he considered, glancing once more toward the backs of their chairs – then such a plan, he decided, just could not include Maggie herself. Remember how she ran across the hall to greet you, he reminded himself. The look of disgust on her face when she had reprimanded her mother. Remember how she had talked of you coming to England too. Of visiting her. Of still being a part of her life.

It should have been enough. Indeed, would have been enough, had a series of occurrences not conspired to capsize that lifeboat and toss the boy back overboard. It began with Miss Florence Matthias taking a moment out of the evening's proceedings to stare quite deliberately in young Eli's direction. It was during the after-dinner address, a moment before Dr. Blaisdell had risen to welcome her esteemed English guest, and then give a brief acknowledgement of Maggie's parents who had come all that way down from the shores of Georgian Bay – a comment that elicited more than a few involuntary chirps of laughter, since most in attendance knew well that Mother Calloway made the trip once every two weeks to audit the progress of her daughter's singing. This was followed by a bit of light but dignified ribbing from Dr. Blaisdell regarding some of her young student's more comical fumblings of a *Pie Jesu* during those lessons (the gist of which, seemingly, required a working knowledge of Latin wordplay).

Then Florence Matthias herself stood and delighted the guests with some tales about luminaries of the classical music world who at one time or another had graced her halls back in Lincolnshire (the gist of which seemingly required knowledge of England's society pages). She followed this by reading a letter. It was, she explained, the first of many letters her dear friend Dr. Enid Blaisdell had sent her, claiming she had found, as she had put it so simply yet pointedly, a *voice*. And while the subsequent body of the letter was careful to mitigate the discovery, claiming the *voice* was still very raw and certainly in need of instruction of the highest limits, it was nonetheless brimming with a clarity and tone that evoked instant emotion from all who heard it. (The gist of which Eli – free from the darkness momentarily – understood perfectly, for he had fallen in love with that voice.) Then, with dollops of mutual respect, both ladies piled tall praises upon one another for their respective roles in Miss Calloway's upcoming musical journey. Matthias to Blaisdell for thinking firstly of her distant academy as being the right choice for this young talent to exercise her potential; Blaisdell to Matthias for trusting her judgment at recognizing Miss Calloway's singular potential in the first place. And so on and so forth. Back and forth … like verbal tennis.

"So once again, on behalf of the faculty here, I would like to thank you for your shared words this evening, Florence. We here in the colonies …"

"Oh Enid … the provinces … please, the provinces. I swear, you make me sound positively like an imperialist."

Chuckles up and down the tables.

"The provinces then. We here rarely are granted the opportunity to meet a musical dignitary such as yourself. So we do wish to thank you for your gracious time this evening and indeed for hosting this event for your new recruit." She attached a bit of a roll of the 'r' on the word recruit, her head shaking back and forth slightly as she broke into a grin. And before the applause that seconded this sentiment had diminished, Florence was back on her feet, calming the affection with palms stretched out downward.

"There is more … if you please … Ladies and Gentlemen, if I could have but a moment more of your time. Thank you."

She cleared her throat, sipped from her water goblet, and then she did it again … Eli was certain, the flash of another completely contemptuous look aimed right at him, for just a split second before she was back addressing her guests and her future pupil with a smile.

"Miss Calloway, given the delightful meetings I had with you and your charming parents this morning, I believe now is the perfect opportunity to inform you here in the presence of your peers and loved ones …" And another look at him … there was no doubt in his mind. "… that your interests would be best served if your tenure at my academy commenced immediately."

It is possible those words may well have been the only trigger needed to release the profound pain Eli Benowitz would feel anew each and every time he revisited the details of that night. However, that surprise announcement was soon trumped twofold by what befell the lad next. There was confirmation of the previous menacing glances, for indeed Matthias did not seem to have the slightest interest in the elation going on around her – Mother Calloway jumping with youthful delight, Bud Calloway rising to his feet and clapping his hands with steely-eyed satisfaction, classmates dancing about and hugging Maggie one by one. No, the esteemed Florence Matthias only stared forward, directly out into the eyes of the only other person in the room who was not celebrating, an unprovable grin of satisfaction seeming to shade her face ever so slightly.

But it was what came after that – the counterpart to this cold-blooded expression – that would prove most crippling. It was an observation occasioned only when Eli broke free of the woman's gaze to look for solace in his true love's eyes. But those eyes were otherwise occupied. They were, in the opinion of everyone else in attendance, back where they belonged, back in focus from a brief and misguided detour. She was bouncing up and down in front of Blaisdell, hugging her mother, then some of the other faculty. Eyes wide with excitement. Eyes of unlimited exuberance. Eyes that, in the midst of that exuberance, had completely forgotten he was there.

~APRIL 1, 1982, SOMETIME PAST MIDNIGHT~

It was all-hands-on-deck to get their new jewel absolutely sparkling on the eve of its maiden concert, so it was well after midnight before Emerson Place was finally clear of the legions of cleaners and decorators, polishers and detailers. Yes there would be security to deal with, of course, but that was no real concern. He had foiled their likes before. What was the negligible prowess of one more part-time security guard? Even two? Once the doors were locked they would no doubt keep to the lobby and the concourses, mostly concerned with their lunch boxes and newspapers, whatever focus they had left over being reserved strictly for sporadic checks of the street entrances, perhaps the loading bay at the back. Due diligence for deterring danger from breaking in. Not at all expecting that it was already inside.

It was finally time. He would get his chance once and for all. Exact his revenge for a life well-ruined. He would make the pain known. Would leave it spread angrily across the brilliant clean plaster of soft eggshell walls; walls whose curvature – the architect in him maintained – was still too gradual in its design to achieve optimal acoustics, given the ceiling's height. "This is supposed to be a concert hall, is it not?" he had implored time and time again … all those days spent watching the construction take shape, aiming his derision at contractors, carpenters, anyone his well-honed loitering skills could get him close to. "Acoustics should be the primary concern, should they not?" he would further expound should he happen to catch the eye of someone who looked the part of the jewel's design team. The suits with the hard hats, they particularly had been his targets.

But that was all over now. The building was up. The ship of perfect design had long since sailed, leaving behind it the unsatisfying sound of his own voice echoing through a sea of deaf ears. All that remained was the scream inside. A scream at a world that had shunned his very existence. It was time for that world to know what it had done. It was time for that world to pay. Damn the freshly polished stage. Damn the plush carpet and the padded seats. Damn the misguided acoustical engineering. The beams and the braces. Hell, damn the very architecture itself. He would condemn it all from top to bottom; from the fine crown moulding to the very support walls that held its skeleton in place. He would fly in the face of the vocation that had once so sustained him. He would abandon it all ... the love of form and function, design and integrity. He would ruin it all with nothing more than mere cosmetics. Let appearance win. Let the winners write their history. Hell, let them write *his* history. He would fight back once and for all with this one final act. He would defile. He would wreck. He would mar. With nothing more than the smear of latex rubbed against and into these pristine, scrubbed-down walls ... these goddamn walls. They didn't want to listen? They would listen now.

He waited for the sound of all four sets of auditorium doors locking before he stirred, emerging from the storage closet behind the far stage-left dressing room – the one he had reserved in his mind ever since the day he noted it on a drafting blueprint the previous fall. He went to work first along the left side-wall of the concert hall, his fist for a brush, wiping the words on in two-foot letters , then three ... repeating the message from front row to last, across the back and up the other side. This was the undeniable conclusion of this shiny new edifice. Of its premiere. Of Handel and his *Messiah*. Of the music that had lured him in only to condemn him for getting too close. Him and his kind! This was their damnable victory, now spread out for all to see. Four-foot letters now as he went around a second time. He climbed up on the arms of the seats, reaching higher and higher up the wall. Maniacally, spastically … grunting … sobbing. The same phrase over and over and over …

Goddamn them. Goddamn them all.

~1987~

"Well, Mr. Page, I finally listened to this song of yours," Maggie announced, lowering herself once again into the chair next to his. Up until her entrance it had been just another Saturday afternoon with the usual regulars, striking their usual lifeless poses along the bar. Just another matinee for the band back on stage as well, the singer leading his usual vain charge. 'Like leading a pep rally at a funeral in here,' he would mutter off-mike at least once per set, usually towards the bass player to his right who, as often as not, was reflecting back the room's sincere disinterest with a glassy stare of his own. The pedal steel player – for his part – kept his head low, staring down his nose towards the strings he so meticulously manoeuvred, like a seamstress finishing off a particularly tricky stitch. On and on they played … old standard after old standard … with scarce any response, let alone appreciation, from the room before them – save for their good friend Murray Page, back again in his usual spot, alone, arms folded over his pint of ale, head up, feet tucked and curled under his chair.

"I think that calls for a drink, don't you?" she called out over top of the opening notes of a country waltz, and when she glanced towards the bar a Jameson was poured. "*Broken Angels.* I made a point last week of remembering the title. Then I had my housekeeper find the recording over in Owen Sound on her last shopping day. Since then, why I must have tried listening to it on half a dozen occasions or more." She paused to address the sets of eyes now glued upon her, glancing again toward the bar until the row of curious regulars spun back to the safety of a baseball game on the TV behind the counter.

"And how can I help you today, Ms. Calloway?" Murray asked with a somewhat laboured sigh.

"Oh come now, Mr. Page. How will we ever get to know each other if you insist on calling me Ms. Calloway and staring off into space like that?"

From the corner of his eye he thought he detected the hint of a grin, and therein, perhaps, a glimpse of her former charm. She leaned in closer.

"You come here to remember her, don't you?" she whispered.

"I come here to have a drink and listen to the boys play," he replied, adding through a swig of his ale, "which is proving difficult at the moment."

"To listen to the boys play your song, don't you mean?"

Murray dropped his glass to the table, turned, and with a long and silent scowl tried vainly to fathom why a woman so proud of her high station in life would choose to step inside a dingy little tavern like this one just to make a game out of his grieving. But before any plausible explanation could present itself, she was up on her feet yelling towards the stage.

"Let's hear *Broken Angels* for my good friend Mr. Murray Page here."

"Stop that," the arena manager hissed, pulling her back into her seat just as the guitar player patronized her with a disingenuous nod.

"It's OK, it's OK. I understand." Her voice trailed off and she reached over to pat the back of his hand with self-amusement that was still – to Murray's mind – foremost in her expression, though after her last outburst it was being tempered by the possibility that the Jameson now being delivered to her table was not her first of the day.

"Did you know your song has a curious melodic passage?" she continued, her hand still draped heavily across his knuckles. "There's a repeated motif in the verse that begins on the dominant, then rises to linger on the tonic before falling into this little three-note figure … *da-de-dah*. It reminds me very much of one of the solos I used to sing in the *Messiah*."

Her eyes floated away toward the dull muted daylight of the grimy windowpanes and she continued to sing the phrase she had described with an effortless clarity that, like her smile a few moments before, also granted Murray a hint of her former glory. Over and over she went, alternating between the text of her beloved aria and the words of the country song. *"I know that my Redeemer liveth … Rest your weary heart my broken little angel …* funny how even a little ditty like this will still borrow from the classics, isn't it? Although I have to say I have trouble imagining it as part of a funeral service."

"Now that's enough!" It was his turn to take to his feet, hands on hips, shaking his head in disbelief. "It's bad enough you coming in here saying this song has been ripped off. But to have the gall–" he stopped short with the realization that his raised voice had turned the bar-side regulars back around to play spectator to the commotion. He began to pace, first down to the men's room door, then back, swallowing a number of gulps of air to try to quell the sudden throb of anger pulsing through his temple, until finally when he felt sufficiently composed, he sat back down in his chair, re-folded his arms – albeit more tightly than usual – and addressed his uninvited guest more calmly.

"First of all … Ms. Calloway," he began again, with intentional formality. "This is my time in here. And so what if I do come in here to remember Helen? It's my life to spend as I see fit. And second of all … how dare you!" He fought back the throb once more. "How dare you march in here and criticize my wife's funeral! Who the hell cares what you think of that song? The boys played it because I asked them to, and I asked them to because that song represents a boatload of good memories. Hell, a lifetime of good memories! And maybe I don't give a rat's ass if it's not the highbrow stuff you made yourself famous singing. But here's the thing: Even though I may not understand your style of music, I still know it's good. I know because I see you teaching Allie and I see how much my granddaughter gets out of it. How it's changed her so much for the good. But maybe that's just the difference between people like you and me. I don't *have* to get it to know that it's important. And I don't *have* to get it to be thankful that it's a part of her life. But just because I don't get it, doesn't give you the right to come in here and make fun of my taste in things."

"Mr. Page, you have it all wrong," she said soberly as she picked at a thread on the hem of her skirt. "I'm not here to belittle you or your–"

"No? Then perhaps you can tell me why the hell you *are* here? 'Cause from where I'm sitting, Lady, that's pretty much all you've done!" He paused again, first for a mouthful of ale, then to wipe his forehead with a napkin. "Just know this, Ms. Calloway," he seethed. "As far as I'm concerned, Helen was way above anything you ever did. Go ahead. Take your finest performance. Your best newspaper review. Your biggest award, or what have you. Wrap 'em all up like one big shiny trophy case to show the world. None of it matters. And you know why? Because all that glory is nothing but a shadow of the woman I lost, *Ms. Calloway* ... So yes, maybe that's why I'm in here every week ... and maybe there's not a day goes by, I–" His voice trailed off hoarsely, his final words catching in his throat. "Surely to God even you can understand that," he mouthed with a gasp, then waited for her reaction which, when it finally arrived, was in fact a curious mix, for, while he did note her nodding in agreement, her faraway expression appeared not so much contrite as preoccupied.

"Yes ... well ... as I believe I was trying to say previously, I did not come in here to aggravate you, Mr. Page," she returned in measured tones, still busy working her fabric. "I have no doubt that you genuinely associate this song with your wife. Perhaps it was a dance you and she shared, or perhaps a particular musical phrase that you heard when she told you she loved you. Of course I understand the importance of things like that. What I was stating was simply an observation based on my life as a singer ... a communicator of lyric and music, Mr. Page. And my observation of *Broken Angels* is that, on its own merits, stripped of the associations and the memories that the song so obviously triggers for you personally, it is a composition primarily of despair and pain … elements with which I think a funeral would already be well supplied. However, since you felt the need to question … let's see … well not only my career, or my ability to empathize with you, but indeed my very character, let me turn the tables and ask you this. If this bar, and these drinks, and this song are indeed a necessary tonic for your loss … then surely *you*, Mr. Page, could entertain the possibility they might be likewise for someone else. Perhaps even someone you insist on seeing as so very different from yourself?"

"What? You're gonna tell me a little country song in the Bluewater Tavern suddenly means the world to you?"

Maggie sat back and shrugged.

"That's rich," Murray scoffed with a chuckle that he immediately regretted, given the speed with which her hand slammed down on the tabletop.

"You do not know me, Sir!" she snapped, her eyes suddenly shiny as she stared down the pointed finger trained on him like the barrel of a gun. "Take my finest performance, you say? Well how should I pick, Mr. Page? Allegedly I had hundreds of them. Thousands even. And my finest reviews? Why, I'll show you scrapbooks full. But why stop there? What about all those silk gowns tailored and altered just for me and my physique? And all the other perks? The dinners at five-star restaurants … on the house. The posh accommodations. Touring weeks and months on end with stays at only the finest of hotels in the finest of cities. Room service. Valet service. Any service a woman could possibly need. Should I go on? The plush broadloom? The king-size beds? The down-filled duvets? The terraces overlooking Manhattan, the Thames, Sydney Harbour?"

"Sounds like a pretty good life to me."

"Except for the one tiny little detail, Mr. Page … what was it you said before? Oh yes … NONE OF IT MATTERED!" There was a second slap of the table and Murray reached to slide his glass to safety. "None of it …" she repeated more calmly, just as the band decided it might be prudent to end their set a song or two early. "Even back in the day, when I was someone closer to the heartless bitch you think I am–"

"I never said anything of the sort!"

"Even then," she reiterated. "None of it mattered. Oh, believe you me, I thought it did. But I was a fool, Mr. Page. And do you know why? Because none of those luxuries turned out to have anything to do with the comforts they were supposed to afford me. They were nothing more than results. Proof that I had achieved and surpassed the goals of all the people who had trained and moulded me. That's the thing about results, Mr. Page. They aren't something that you enjoy or appreciate. In the end they're just things you chase, then achieve, then scratch off the list of your life's tasks. But chase them I did. After all, what good is the proof of my success if it's not understood by everyone involved? Agents and concert presenters. PR people. The orchestras, the accompanists. The poor assistants hired to look after my daily needs. My career was *a voice*, and *a voice* only, Mr. Page. Why, my instructors said as much the very first day they picked me to go off to England to study. '*We have discovered a voice,*' they said. Not a singer. Not Maggie Calloway. Just *a voice*. To them I was merely its keeper; a babysitter entrusted with its care … and, as they loved to remind me, not a particularly good one at that. *The voice* was their prize. It was the trophy for their teaching careers. Not me."

She grabbed her drink and winced in preparation for a particularly large mouthful, then returned both her eyes and her finger to Murray. "You know what the royal suite at a five-star hotel is, Mr. Page?" she demanded. "It's a door, followed by ten steps, then a bed, a sitting area, a window, then the end of your universe." Another gulp. "But you were right, Mr. Page. It does sound like a good life. So who should I complain to? Who would lend me a fair ear? You? I don't think so. You look at me and see one thing and one thing only. Just like everybody else. So go ahead. Tell me how you would describe me. Aloof? Pompous? No, go ahead. I've heard so many damn variations frankly I don't give a damn anymore myself. But for whatever it's worth, maybe those descriptions don't quite hit the mark. At the end of the day, maybe I'm just somebody who could use a drink in a place like this. Just … like … you!"

Murray shook his head once more. "Who'da thunk it? The great Margaret Calloway sitting around the Bluewater Tavern with a bunch of tired old farts?"

"Goddamn it!" This time both hands struck the veneer. "The great Margaret Calloway is a tired old fart!" And she was on her feet once again, faster than he would have guessed she could move. "I thought it would be different in here," she muttered. "I thought it would at least be … forgiving. Clearly I thought wrong. Good day."

~DECEMBER 11, 2010~

Allison glanced over at the elderly woman to monitor her state. Gone were the impromptu conducting and the murmurs of instruction. Gone too were the fluid hand motions and the serenity of the first act. True, her eyes were still closed, but her head was now slightly bowed and it was very still.

He was despised and rejected of men
A man of sorrows and acquainted with grief
He hid not his face from shame and spitting

Most would have thought the woman sleeping, but Allison knew otherwise. She knew the early cycles of the Second Movement were not her mentor's preference. She remembered how Maggie had always rather cryptically commented on the *isolation* inherent in the text. How it required a rising crescendo of tension, even pain, on the part of the soloist. How it was a duty ... a necessary evil, she called it.

~1987~

She did come back. Each and every Saturday afternoon for the next six weeks, over which time they cultivated a mutually tolerable silence, sitting alone, side by side, sipping their ale and whiskey, listening to the band and humming along whenever *Broken Angels* turned up on the set list. Occasionally they would fill the space with small doses of safe and easy talk. The weather. The taste of their respective drinks. Allison's lessons. Then they would retreat into the solitude of their own thoughts, Murray for his part pondering the less easy, less safe matters still left unspoken. The question of why this woman would insist on coming there. Why would she ever have thought it might be a *forgiving* place? And, of course, the question at the heart of his curiosity: What exactly was it that she needed to be *forgiven* for?

It was during her eighth visit, well towards the end of summer, and not coincidentally just as the final chord of Murray Page's favourite song rang off the band's instruments, that the answers finally began to trickle out of her.

"You know, that wood finish on the facing of the bar over there reminds me a great deal of the panelling back in the rehearsal hall at Lincoln Academy," she began, out of nowhere.

"How's that?"

"So many details of that cursed place ... still right there, you know?" she mumbled, tapping a finger to her temple, her eyes locked on the woodwork.

"You can remember the panelling?"

"I can. I can remember the panelling," she frowned. "And how scuffed the floor always looked. That always puzzled me. So beat-up for such a supposedly renowned place. Oh, and the room had this close dank smell. Lord, how I grew to loathe that smell. You know, in my whole time there I can't recall a single window ever being so much as cracked open."

She leaned back, pressed her palms together, and brought her fingertips up to rest on her chin. "I had a tyrant for an instructor, you know. The insufferable Dame Florence Matthias. Day after day of breathing exercises and scales and drills. *'A soloist should always exude poise throughout the enterprise of any vocal delivery, Miss Calloway, lest an audience become preoccupied with whatever heaving or gasping she might inadvertently impose onto a composer's musical intentions.'* Do you know it was weeks before we even touched an actual sheet of music? Mind you," she chuckled, "once we did, it proved just as much a struggle. *'I'm afraid your intuitive attempts at phrasing will only get you so far around here, Miss Calloway.'* That was a bit of a constant refrain for poor old Matthias when it came to her *'talented yet provincially impulsive'* student."

"Sounds like a bit of a snob."

"No *bit* about it, Mr. Page, although I will admit I was something of a handful even back then. I can recall one lesson when I dared question her interpretation of a particular phrase from Verdi. I received a bit of a tirade for that indiscretion, I'm afraid. But I went right back at her, demanding to know why we should even bother to refer to the lesson as *musical interpretation* when all I was being asked to do was mimic the directions of someone who claimed to know the one and only manner in which Verdi should be sung. I believe the phrase 'like a trained seal' may have even come out of my mouth."

Murray let out a chuckle. "And how'd that go over?"

"*'Oh ... I'm sorry, Miss Calloway. Have we switched places? Have my years of interpretation been trumped so completely by the young farm girl from Ontario?'* She would always find a way to work in the word *Ontario* into any reprimand. She'd draw it out from between her lips, with a slight roll on the 'r' that, believe me, conveyed the woman's opinion of the colonies in no uncertain terms."

"Charming."

"Well, like I said, I was a bit of a handful. And I was three months pregnant by then, thank you very much. All that morning sickness would get anybody a little bit cranky," she chuckled. "Not that Old Lady Matthias took any of that into account. I believe we went back to another four days of arpeggios after that particular outburst. Trust me, from then on, I swallowed everything the woman fed me and spat it back out without even making a face. *'I have shepherded a generation of soloists through these halls, Miss Calloway.'* ... Yes, Miss Matthias ... *'If attention to detail and precision cannot be exercised in the most rudimentary scale, then it will not be present on the concert stage, Miss Calloway.'* ... Yes, Miss Matthias ... *'I am your Lord. You shall have no other god before me.'* ... Yes, Miss Matthias ..."

Her voice trailed away, fading into soft laughter, followed by a glissando of a sigh, then the slow burn of Irish whiskey. "All that regurgitation," she mumbled, shaking her head. "All that clinical dissection of the mechanics of singing. Tricks and pointers on how to convey the emotion and the depth of a particular musical passage without having to be really subject to it yourself. At the end of day, that's all she was really about."

Maggie closed her eyes, raised the index finger of her right hand, and while gently conducting the air in front of her, sang in a musical whisper:

A man of sorrows and acquainted with grief
He hid not his face from shame and spitting

The words lingered between them for a second and then her eyes reopened as she suddenly sensed his perplexed expression. She nodded, straightened her shoulders and -- as he now realized she always did when collecting herself -- began smoothing out the folds in her attire.

"Very well," she continued matter-of-factly, "you have questions."

Murray Page held up a hand. "Nope ... somebody else's personal life isn't anything of my business, I'm just here to have a drink and–"

But he was cut short. Interrupted by her hand taking his. And by a pleading, faintly desperate look he had not seen from her before.

"Please," she stated softly. "I've tried to leave it all in the past. Lord knows I've tried ..."

Carefully he took her hand and set it back in her lap, but feeling sufficiently permitted to inquire, folded his arms across his chest – as she now noticed he always did when collecting his thoughts – and leaned back in his chair, a squint of concentration passing over his face.

"Well ..." he drawled out slowly, "I guess I'm just a little confused about the timing of what you were saying."

Maggie nodded. "You are an observant man, Mr. Page."

"I mean, I just would have assumed you were all finished with your schooling by the time your daughter came along. So when you mentioned being pregnant and having to do your lessons ..." He paused.

"Go on," she quietly permitted. "Please ... finish the thought."

"Well, you said you were just starting out with that Academy, but you were already, you know ... with child. So I'm just thinking it must not have left a lot of time to meet your husband and get married and have a daughter–"

"That's because I wasn't yet pregnant with Christine, Mr. Page. And my marriage to Russell was still five years off." She watched as the layers of realization washed across the arena manager's face like fresh coats of paint.

"So if you had just nicely arrived over there–" he started.

Maggie nodded.

"So you got pregnant ... over here?"

"Very good, my friend," she said lifting her glass. "And the times being as they were, that little predicament was shame enough for the powers that be to ship me all the way across the ocean as quickly as possible to have it taken care of."

Murray shook his head. "Well, I'm confused again then," he said. "I thought you went over there to study singing?"

"Two birds with one stone, Mr. Page, two birds with one stone. It was a favour from Matthias to one of my teachers in Toronto. There was a clinic, you see. Very private. Very discreet. Just a train ride away … down into London once my time was right."

She sagged to the back of her chair. "I was to go alone. Just me and my suitcase … personal effects, toiletries … I can still picture the leaflet they gave me so clearly … there's another memory that's still right there. It was on pale green paper … very matter-of-fact with its instructions …" Her voice trailed away once more, her eyes making a hastened retreat to the wood grain of the barnboard wall, just as she felt the first moist trail begin its path down her cheeks.

"Oh heavens … just look at me," she scolded herself, fumbling vainly in her purse for any sign of a tissue until Murray snapped to attention and slid over his drink napkin, which she accepted with instant relief, mouthing a silent thank-you before continuing.

"Do you remember the first time I visited you in here?" she asked. "You wanted to know if I was a religious person, because I had become so well-known for singing the *Messiah*?"

Murray squirmed awkwardly in his chair.

"No, you needn't worry about it. I found it a very interesting question. In fact I've been thinking about it a great deal lately. And just like the wood panels over there … oh hell, who's kidding who … much more than the wood panels over there, this had me remembering my early days back in England. You see, as it turned out, the very same year I arrived at Lincoln Academy, the school was selected to perform *Messiah* for a BBC broadcast and recording, the same recording that's on the album I lent to Allison. And out of nowhere Matthias picks me for the aria *I Know That*

My Redeemer Liveth – the one that sounds like your country song in fact ... even though I was supposedly just the new student *from the colonies* ... even though I still wasn't doing much more than scales and breathing exercises for the old hag up until that point ... and even though I was scheduled for my dreaded procedure only four days later. I tell you, that's when I learned my place. That's when I learned I was merely keeper of the *voice*. Not the *voice* itself. Because it became very apparent in no uncertain terms that all anyone around me cared about ... I mean really cared about ... was that damn concert. '*Purity of tone, Miss Calloway, we need purity of tone.*' I ask you, what the hell did I have to sound so pure about? I was damaged goods. I was putting in time waiting for my day to abort a life and all the while there's old Matthias with her little baton and her clumpy old shoes, pacing back and forth across the rehearsal hall, demanding that some virtuous sound come bursting out of me. Do you see the hypocrisy of it all, Mr. Page? The utter farce?"

Murray leaned across to the next table to retrieve several more drink napkins, surmising their need by the cracking in her voice. She grabbed the stack from him and immediately blew her nose. "And I know what you're going to say. 'Isn't this the way things were taken care of back then?' And you would be correct. Why, we weren't killing a fetus, were we? We weren't scraping a womb. Not back in 1951. No sir, we were merely tending to a little matter. Merely dealing with a little mistake."

She blew again before going on. "And my mother was completely complicit in the whole affair. She only agreed to the procedure ... say, there's another conveniently palatable term, isn't it? ... the *procedure* ... anyway, she only agreed because it had been a condition of my scholarship at the academy in the first place. And it had been decided that the procedure – Jesus and Mary, I can't stop, can I? – the *abortion* ... there I said it ... the abortion would take place some weeks after I arrived, safely before I started to really show beyond what could be explained away as an over-indulgence in English cooking I suppose. And upon its completion there was the understanding that no one was to speak of it again. The door for potential stigma was to be locked and sealed for good."

"For good. Right," she heard his voice from inside the rim of his glass and waited for him to expand on the comment. But Murray Page was a product of times past as well, so the chances of his discussing the details of an abortion – albeit details that Maggie herself showed no signs of slowing down for – in anything more than *palatable* terms were next to none.

"Anyway," she continued after a moment, "as the time approached I began to grow restless. It seemed like I had just nicely settled into my lodgings. My landlady was a gentle woman who kept a very nice little room for me without unduly infringing upon it. So the thought of leaving that safety for the trip to London ... well it grew more and more dreadful every day. I was to go down by train ... first to King's Cross ... then a taxi up to Shoreditch. Just me and my overnight bag ... with the prescribed necessities from my little green leaflet ... change of nightgown, robe, slippers ... I was to simply knock on the door ..." She lunged for the wad of napkins once more. "You know, the pamphlet said there would be some lingering pain. By God, they sure nailed that one, didn't they!"

Murray watched as she went through tissue after tissue, dabbing at the corners of her bloodshot eyes, patting her flushed cheeks and her reddened nose. "And what about the father?" he asked as gently as he could.

"Ah yes, I was waiting for you to get around to that," she said with a sniff, and in abject defeat she closed her eyes and dropped her arms to her sides, letting the remaining napkins fall where they may.

"His name was Eli Benowitz," she sighed. "A Jewish boy ... which shouldn't have mattered ... even back then. But–"

"But it did," Murray finished, eyes firmly on his own glass.

"It just all happened so fast," she whispered, shaking her head. "One day I was accepted to the Academy and I'm chock full of all these grand plans; how he would come and visit me before classes began so we could tour about together. London, the Cotswolds, down to the seaside. Then the next day I find out I'm carrying his child …"

"What did he say when you told him?"

She wanted to look up, to meet his eyes and plead in the face of the inquisitive stare she knew was now hard-trained on her, but she just couldn't. Her eyes defaulted instead to her glass as she let a fresh sip of whiskey splay across her tongue and settle into the edges of her throat.

"You mean you never told him?"

She bobbed her head hard and through a blur of tears went back to work on her hem.

"Well …" Murray stumbled, clearing his throat and shifting his weight back and forth. "Well it's understandable I guess," he said nervously. "Like you said, such were the times, weren't they. I mean, I imagine your folks would have probably just read him the riot act, wouldn't they? Like they probably did to you, I would guess–"

"That's the shame of it," she sobbed. "No one had to. Not my parents, not my professors at St. Timothy's, not Matthias. Because I and my stupid star-struck eyes unwittingly played the role of accomplice to perfection. And by the time we had been through all my send-offs in Toronto … why the newspaper there even ran a picture of Mother and me boarding the ship for the ride across the Atlantic … well, after all that attention let's just say all those initial plans for Eli had long since faded away. And the only travelling I did was with Mother right by my side every waking hour of the day. She stayed the first two weeks to see me settled in, you see."

"More like, keep an eye on ya would be my guess," Murray grunted.

"Indeed," she agreed, a faint but decidedly cynical grin edging out from the corner of her mouth. "Oh we did take in London. Buckingham Palace, Westminster, Piccadilly … the usual highlights for a first-timer's visit. Tried to get to the Royal Albert and the other big concert halls, a good number of which were still being reconstructed from the war, mind you. But I must say the degree of damage wasn't nearly as devastating as what we saw during our week on the continent. Mother hired a car and a tour guide to show us through Belgium and northern France, you see. The poor thing turned out to be quite preoccupied with showing us every example of bombed-out rubble she could find. More concerned with what had been lost than what had stayed up, it seemed. And the memorials! Sweet Jesus, I think we saw every commemoration going. Ypres, Passchendaele, Vimy."

"Those were from the First World War," Murray noted.

"Indeed they were. They were also all Canadian in origin, which we eventually surmised was the point. It seems our guide was attempting to cater to Mother's and my sense of national pride. She, being Dutch, kept referring to us as her liberators, which I confess even back then sounded a bit too over the top, bless her heart."

She paused for another sip. "I do remember one thing, though," she said with a squint. "I remember how she proudly told us about the ground on which most all of these memorials sat. How they had been deeded to the government of Canada as sovereign land. Did you know that?"

Murray shook his head.

"Nor did I. But apparently it's true. If you go over there and stand in front of the Vimy Memorial today your feet are officially on Canadian soil."

Murray nodded. "And why not? Nobody else could take that ridge 'til our boys showed up."

"If you say so, Mr. Page. I'm afraid I'm still rather unschooled when it comes to the details of our military history. But I will say this. If an event's impact is measured by the quality of the monument that commemorates it, then I concur, the battle of Vimy Ridge must have been a very important victory." Her eyes fell closed again. "He would have just loved it."

"Who?"

"Eli."

This time Murray squinted. "The father?"

"He was studying to be an architect. Did I mention that before? Perhaps not. Anyway, I just know he would have admired the Vimy Memorial. It would have very much appealed to his philosophy of what a structure should be. I mean it was just so stunning … those clear bright stone columns reaching up out of the earth, stretching to the sky, holding up images of figures depicting the highest virtues of humanity … truth, valour, justice. That sort of thing. Then at the bottom there's the sculpture showing a soldier's tomb … and nearby another of a young woman grieving. The guide said she represented the new country of Canada mourning the loss of her men, but I don't know … to me she looked like a mother."

Murray watched as she rose from her seat and began to pace in front of their table, stopping a few times to stare silently at him, as if sizing up his worthiness as an audience for any further details of her story. Then it was back and forth again, after a few passes grabbing her drink to take with her. Two steps, stop and pivot. Sip. Two more steps.

"On the day of my procedure," she began without breaking stride, "I awoke early, and since I still had a few hours before the train to London, I decided to wander up to Lincoln Cathedral. It's a frightfully trying walk from where I was lodging, straight up the hill on this treacherously steep cobbled street that makes its way up to the old walled portion of the city. Quite a workout for a pregnant woman, let me say. My landlady allowed it. I think she was under the impression I was going there to attempt some sort of eleventh-hour appeal for forgiveness."

"Not the case?"

She shook her head. "The truth is, Mr. Page, I have never found cathedrals to be a particularly forgiving place. Grand, yes. Great for singing in, too. But as for forgiving …"

"Why'd you go then?"

"That is, as they say, the million-dollar question. And to this day I have no answer, other than to say it proved to be one of the most important things I ever did. You see, Lincoln Cathedral is quite an impressive place. It was built back in the late twelfth century – well, expanded really; a church of some description had already been there for over a century or two. But under the direction of a beloved bishop named Saint Hugh … friendly sort of a name don't you think? Anyway, under his watchful eye it was transformed into this massive Gothic Cathedral. Some think it may have been the tallest structure in all of Europe at the time … perhaps even the whole world. And as I was saying, it sits high alongside the old castle walls and overlooks not just the city of Lincoln but I dare say a good portion of the shire as a whole."

Murray leaned forward onto his forearms and considered the picture she was describing. "Well, I imagine that's how a lot of those really old cities got started way back then," he reasoned. "You know, spreading out from some big church or castle or what have you."

"Yes, well unfortunately not all of Lincoln's urban sprawl can be assigned simply to population expansion, Mr. Page. That's one of the first things I learned on my walk that morning."

"I'm sorry. I don't follow."

"About halfway up the hill I stopped to catch my breath, as it turns out, right in front of two very old buildings that had signs over their doors that dated them even further back in the twelfth century, in fact decades before St. Hugh decided to put his city on the map with the world's biggest church. Back when all that dull old stone along the castle wall, I dare say, would have still been looking quite spiffy and new. Yet here are these buildings just as old, way down the side of the hill, away outside the safety of those castle walls. It was the names on those signs above their doorways that told me why. *Jews House* and *Jews Court*. Seems that was as close a welcome as they were going to get back then."

"Now wait a minute. You can't be certain–"

"Maybe not on my way up," she snapped back, coming to a full stop. "But let's just say by the time I finally made it to the top my mind had been pretty well made up. And even if there was still any doubt lingering after that, it was completely taken care of on the trip back down. You see, I had just wanted to find a quiet spot, but the Cathedral was so damned busy that morning … people coming and going, an organist rehearsing some ghastly fugue … cleaning staff working away. I ended up just standing in the middle of what they call the Angel Choir, daydreaming in front of the tomb of good old St. Hugh himself."

"Sorry, what kinda choir?"

"Oh. I'm speaking architecturally now, Mr. Page. The choir of a cathedral. It's the open area between the altar and the nave."

Another squint.

"Where the congregation and the choir would be."

"Oh."

"Now in Lincoln's case, that area is simply huge, with these vast vaulted arches hundreds of feet in the air. And like everywhere else, it turned out to be anything but peaceful. School groups, church groups, tour groups. They all just kept traipsing by one after another. And all the tour guides were particularly keen to show off a new plaque that had been erected for someone named Little Saint Hugh."

"The bishop's son?"

"Not back in those good old Catholic days, my friend. No. As it turns out, no relation at all. But he was no less influential as far as the Cathedral was concerned. You see Little Hugh lived somewhere back in those 1200s and actually died when he was only nine years old. Apparently his body was found in the well by the Jew House, so it was presumed he had drowned at the hands of the residents there. One man was tried and executed. Ninety others of the Jewish persuasion were rounded up and imprisoned. A good number of them were also killed. The good news was the boy's death made him something of a celebrity, what with so many of the fine Christian faithful of the day viewing him as a martyr, viewing his remains therefore as a talisman of sorts for miraculous healings. Well the Cathedral soon realized the pilgrimage possibilities, excellent marketers as they were, even back then, so they confiscated the boy's bones, enshrined them alongside their beloved bishop, and watched the traffic flow. People would flock from all over to be healed of their maladies, and as part of their homage to the poor innocent lad, they would unleash their wrath against the dirty Zionist murderers who surely were the cause of not only this atrocity, but every other evil that had befallen the earth, right back to Jesus on the cross. The plaque had been put up the year before as an apology for the church's part in perpetuating such witch hunts. And you know, to this day I can still see those last lines so clearly ... just as if I'm still right there in front of them.

> *Lord forgive what we have done*
> *Amend what we are*
> *Direct what we shall be*

"I couldn't help thinking of Eli. I couldn't help wondering how the architecture would have struck him, had he been standing there with me before the chancel of one of the finest examples of English Gothic design, below the cut and polished stone of a tower the height of the Great Pyramids of Egypt."

"And what did you decide?"

"Nothing, I'm afraid. And at any rate, these were just the musings of someone in denial, Mr. Page. Like I said, it was when I was on my way back down the hill, back past the Jewish buildings once again, that it hit me with full force." Her voice broke once more and she lunged for the last bar napkin, scrunching it tightly in her hand before it even reached her eyes. "It was like ... like I was right back there again, you know?"

"Back up in the Cathedral?"

"No."

"I'm sorry, back where then?" Murray interjected, his hands now on his knees as he perched on the edge of his chair.

"Vimy, Mr. Page. Vimy."

More squinting.

"You see, there was one other historical tidbit our little Dutch girl told us about, but only after she had exhausted all the other virtuous accounts of the place. And, I should add, it was something she offered with a considerable scowl across her face. Like it was a job requirement that was otherwise against her will. Understandable, really."

"I'm sorry again, but I'm just not following–"

"I'm talking about a little event called World War II, Mr. Page!" she lashed out suddenly. "Perhaps you heard about it on the news. How the Nazis blitzed their way right through a little neighbourhood known as Europe!"

"Now hang on–"

"No, you hang on. Those bastards blew up and burned everything in their path," she spewed. "I know. I saw the remains. Churches and schools and homes. Homes that cradled lives, Mr. Page. Flesh and Blood. Children and Babies."

He wanted to retaliate. How dare this coddled woman, this mere *singer* … someone whose biggest hardship in life was probably a sore throat or a loose thread on some gown … how dare she lecture him on The War! Him, whose father served in WWI, whose town had lost three men at Ypres alone. But before his indignation could organize itself in any coherent manner, she was back marching anew, glass in hand, her drink swishing from rim to rim.

"Don't you find it curious, Mr. Page, that the Germans knocked everything they saw to kingdom come except that goddamn beautiful monument? It's true! It turns out that when Old Adolph came racing through northern France, he had something of an epiphany when he happened upon good old Vimy. Seems those latent artistic sensibilities of his kicked in, because he thought it was just about the most beautiful thing he had ever seen. Rumour has it he even ordered his own SS Guard to stand vigil and protect the place from his own attacks."

Her voice had grown loud, cracking and peaking with a most unmusical emotion. She paced faster, her hands reaching from chair to chair to help with her balance as she picked up speed. "Can you believe it? Hitler and Canada. Canada and Hitler … in perfect agreement." She stopped to drain the remains of her glass, the final fuel for the confession she had so needed to have someone hear.

"And there's stupid me. Standing around, bawling like a calf on the side of a hill. Bawling away like some fool trying to touch the bones of a dead child so as to walk again, or regain sight. Only in my case, there's no ailment. No disability. I'm strictly there to ensure I fulfill my calling. To raise *the voice* to the heights it was destined to climb. There I am standing around … standing around just like the world stood around while that Nazi bastard tried to obliterate a whole race. There I am … Just me and Adolph, standing there enjoying the scenery with a goddamn oven for a womb!"

She slammed her glass to the table and scrambled for her purse, but caught her ankle on one of the standard-issue chair legs, and landed in a heap on the dusty barroom floor. Vainly Murray lunged to save her, but she was already down. "NO … This was a mistake!" she cried out. "I can't … I CAN'T!" And with swipes of her arm warding off all attempts at assistance, she staggered to her feet and to the silent stares of the lifeless room stumbled out the door.

~DECEMBER 11, 2010~

Towards the end of the Second Part she began to moan – a low, barely-audible sound first noticed between the harpsichord's final cadence of the tenor recitative, slightly ahead of the strident bow strokes of the violins leading into the subsequent aria …

Thou shalt break them with a rod of iron …

"I can't … no …" she whimpered, and rocked from side to side, her fingertips pulling at the fabric of her armrests as if she were trying to rip them aside, as if they were bars blocking her escape.

"Maggie, what is it? What's wrong?" Allison whispered, turning quickly to attend to her friend. But she had been beaten to the task from the other side. With a steel-eyed told-you-so stare aimed right back at her, she watched as Christine slowly began to peel her mother's hands from the upholstery one finger at a time. Once they were extricated she pressed them firmly back onto the elderly woman's lap and held them there tightly.

"Mother, it's me – Christine," she hissed just below the swell of strings, her words – much like her actions – sounding more like restraint than concern. "You're fine, Mother. We're at the *Messiah*. It's almost intermission."

~APRIL 1, 1982, SOMETIME PAST MIDNIGHT~

What had he done? Oh God, what the hell had he done? He stared panting in front of his mural of hatred, with the impact of his actions hitting him head-on, and suddenly his will was gone, replaced by waves of remorse washing over his paint-soaked body until he sagged to the carpet and heaved the contents of his stomach onto the freshly-laid carpet.

This was his fate, then. To live and die with the certitude of despair, no matter which way he turned. Either wallow in the torture of a life that had betrayed him, or wallow in the regret of having lashed back. It didn't matter anymore. Blame was everywhere and nowhere, within and without. He could take it no longer. He picked up his paint can and hurled it as far as he could, an angry crimson trail arcing through the air and splattering against the fresh varnish of the concert stage with a crash. The explosion of sound, both from the impact and from his cries of anguish that had sent it reeling, set off a flurry of activity from the lobby outside, with choruses of 'What the hell was that?' followed by the scrambling scratches of keys in locks.

And just like that, with the threat of recrimination but a door away, his resolve returned, fuelled afresh. In a flash he was on his feet, darting for the shadows of the stage wings, back past the storage area that had previously concealed him – that would be of no use now – back through the maze of dressing rooms, carpentry workshops, electrical rooms, washrooms and closets. He would not be caught, he promised himself. Could not be caught. Not after coming this far.

Triumphantly, his mind flashed back through the succession of exploits that his powers of elusiveness had facilitated over the years. On two continents, no less … file rooms and archives … hospital storages, halls of records … the clinic back in England. A parade of memories led him back – just as it always did – to his very first trespass, to that initial violation that had justified all those that followed. It was a modest old farmhouse, out on the shore road just east of Wiarton. He had sneaked through an open window while husband and wife snored soundly upstairs. There, he found all he needed … stuffed away in the desk drawer by the phone in the hallway: correspondence from mother to daughter, daughter to mother, and, most damningly, Lincoln Academy to mother and daughter alike. It was subterfuge. It was willful interference, deliberate deceit.

And just as always, whenever this memory was revisited, so too did the anger return. He raced back through the darkened bowels of the concert hall with the speed of forgotten youth, diving headlong for the dumpster just inside the loading bay doors, full of discarded two-by-fours and old piping once used for temporary bracing and makeshift scaffolds. Materials no longer needed now that the great Emerson Place was up and standing on her own.

He was glad once more. Glad he did what he did. Sorry only he hadn't done more. Shocked them more. Damaged them more. *Fuck them all,* he concluded as he lay amidst the heap of expendable rubble. *Fuck the hall. And opening night ... and her. Fuck her. Once and for all.*

~SUMMER 1951~

She is alone at the cottage door, double-checking the address on the pamphlet against the number on the otherwise unadvertised building. She has just raised her hand to knock when the quiver starts, first in her knuckles, then through her arms and shoulders and deep into her. She watches in horrified amazement as she slowly realizes the tension that she has been storing inside. Gone are the handlers, the fiddlers and the manipulators. Gone are the so-called shapers of her future – parents, teachers, supposed guardians. She is alone. She is completely alone.

She would now become one of *those* women, the kind her mother and her aunts used to talk about with head-shaking whispers at the hair salon, or after church, or during their weekly quilting bees. She had not known at the time what it was that caused such disdain in their voices, nor why they would mumble and quickly change the subject once they became aware that little Maggie was listening in. But now here she stood, ready to descend to those very depths that her family had decried. Fallen from the radiant heights of the concert stage where her mother, from the time she had given birth to little Maggie, had dreamed she would climb. Fallen to the depths of a camouflaged cottage in a town and a country that was not her own, standing in the drizzle, carrying a tenant of her own. What dreams had anyone for this life? This would-be *procedure.* What thoughts for this voiding of matter and space ... this impediment to the dreams and desires that had been begotten during her own gestation, twenty-one years before?

~DECEMBER 11, 2010~

"Isn't this exactly what I said would happen?" Christine hissed. "Isn't it?"

"What's wrong? Is it her medication?"

"You tell me. You're the self-appointed authority when it comes to my mother."

"Well, what's she trying to say?"

"Who knows? The only thing that's clear is that this hare-brained idea of yours was obviously too much for her. We're leaving after the Hallelujah!"

"Maybe if we walked her around the concourse at the break. Or a breath of fresh air–"

"No. We're through with this, Allison. We're through!"

~APRIL 1, 1982~

The noise and confusion swelled as the night watchmen rallied into action, their efforts soon augmented by the sounds of sirens, and then the police – the dancing beams of their flashlights probing every nook and cranny before eventually subsiding as their attention turned back to consider with disgust the degree of damage inflicted on the theatre's virgin walls.

He lay silently, listening to how their voices called out in agreement about the seriousness of the words, the vitriol – the hatred that must have occasioned them. Listened as they discussed the need for a reinforcement of security, and the need to inform everyone concerned – the concert hall staff, the manager … 'Wake up the mayor,' he heard one officer command. They would have to talk to the orchestra and choir as well, they reasoned.

The conductor too, and the soloists. He lay in silent satisfaction until all of these voices had had their say, had exhausted themselves of every theory and every contingency they could come up with. And still he lay, completely inert, until the restless night gave way to dawn and the furor of their awful discovery began to merge slowly with the unassuming morning sounds of the city. He listened for the garbage truck to pull up behind the bay doors, for workers to slide open those doors, 'wave her' back to pick up Emerson's remaining debris. Waited for the inevitable delay of duties while salutations were exchanged, cigarettes lit, coffees stirred and sipped. Then, with everyone around him sufficiently preoccupied, he gently lifted himself out of the receptacle and slid out a side door into the early sun of what he could not but note was an unusually warm morning for the first day of April.

His initial stop was the public fountains of Allen Park to wash the caked-on latex evidence from his hands. But once there, something in the task started to gnaw at him until suddenly he realized that just like his well-scrubbed knuckles and forearms, so too would his efforts back at the hall soon be eradicated – and most likely before anyone else would ever see it, take it in fully, reel from its curse. Why, it could very well already be painted over, he surmised, the walls once again pure and homogenized. Like it had never even happened. He paced about the concrete bowl, scattering the early-morning pedestrians to wide berths with his agitated gate. He needed to think. He needed to correct this possibility. He paced faster, more urgently … then with a kick and splash and a shout of satisfaction, he hit upon a course of action.

He would go to his locker and get the money. Yes, his ever-so-carefully rolled-up bounty that he counted and recounted each and every day. He would tally once more, just to be sure. And if there was still enough – he only needed to borrow one quarter after all – he would make known what he did. He would ensure someone would write it down. Keep it as a matter of record. File it as noteworthy. And he would make the call from his favourite booth, the one at the south end of Markham Street ... with the high brick wall right behind it. Yes, he would dial one final time. Hear the greeting that had been his crutch for so many years.

Distress Line ... how can I help you?

~DECEMBER 11, 2010~

Heads from the row in front of them now turned to locate the source of the distraction. "Damn it, Mother," her daughter muttered, once again wrestling with the woman's hands, this time trying to pin them under her own knees, the act of immobilization only serving to launch Maggie's legs into motion ... folding and unfolding, twisting to break free.

"No ... I can't!" she moaned. "I can't!"

~SUMMER 1951~

By the time the door creaks open – the attendant having only been warned of a guest by the growing sobs emanating from the stoop outside – she is but a sprinting figure, diminishing into the rainy fog of a cold afternoon, her carefully-packed suitcase flailing along behind her.

~SEPTEMBER 1951~

Dear Mrs. Calloway,

I am writing as a matter of record to spell out the terms and conditions of the contingency plan that was agreed upon in principle via telegram earlier this week. Given your daughter's sudden decision to carry her child through to term, papers have been signed to compel her to release the baby for adoption immediately upon its birth. The delay that this will cause in Maggie's vocal studies will be – as we have discussed – offset by a partial forfeiture of your daughter's scholarship. Please note that payment of the amount of said forfeiture will be required at your earliest opportunity. This will serve to reserve a deferred spot in the school for the following term.

Also, per our discussions, please note that we have impressed upon your daughter that any further deviation on her part will result in a complete nullification of the scholarship and her immediate expulsion from Lincoln Academy. I have enclosed, for your records, the revised code of conduct that has already been stipulated to Maggie.

Regards
Florence Matthias
Lincoln Voice Academy

What followed was taken, in large measure, from the original set of regulations that had been sent when Maggie first received acceptance into the academy, the only difference being that the portions dealing with fraternization had now been underlined for particular consideration. Only the final point – point number seventeen – served as any actual amendment, handwritten as it was across the bottom of the page, an obvious contingency specific to Maggie and Maggie alone. But it was one that her mother and father readily endorsed, and one with which the young soloist herself was by then in no condition to be anything other than compliant. She was, after all, beginning to feel the child's growing weight straining the muscles in her back. Beginning to wonder if the nausea and sickness that she had been promised would alleviate after a few weeks would actually ever subside. Beginning to feel the burden of her decision to give the ever-defining mass of bone and tissue inside her its due.

The amendment was brief and directly to the point.

(17) **There shall be no attempts to contact the baby's father.**

~1987~

"Your friend not in today?" the pedal steel player inquired, pausing on his way toward the stage for the band's first set.

Murray glanced up to catch the young man's eye, and once satisfied the comment hadn't been made at his expense, shook his head and returned to his beer. "Nope," he said quietly.

"Ally still getting lessons from her?"

Murray nodded.

"Well good on you, Mr. Page. I mean Margaret Calloway was … well, she was the best. I mean the top shelf. So, good on you for getting that kind of talent for your granddaughter. And good for you for listening to her last week, too. Looked like she was pretty worked up about something, but obviously you were taking the time to lend an ear."

Part of him wanted to say thanks, and in some way to take a bit of credit for doing just that, but blocking the way was the need for some degree of deniability … or at least the perception that he hadn't actually got as caught up in her story as he had … that he had just been doing a favour sipping drinks with her every weekend for the last two months.

"Oh, and I've been meaning to tell you," the young man continued, pulling up a chair to straddle backwards. "That was pretty fascinating what you mentioned to me a few weeks back. That thing you said Ms. Calloway noticed about *Broken Angels* and the *Messiah*."

Another nod. But only one.

"I mean when you first told me, I thought to myself … no way. But then it kept gnawing away at me for the rest of the afternoon, so I went home and pulled out my own recording. Montreal Philharmonic and the Dumont Chorus."

"You listen to that stuff?" Murray broke his silence with a start.

It was the young man's turn to nod. "Absolutely. I was weaned on it in fact. Mozart, Bach, Elgar and Vivaldi. My mom was a piano teacher, see. Accompanied the community choir in my hometown back east. Probably the biggest reason I took my degree in music at Western."

"I'll be damned," the arena manager muttered.

"Actually I like all kinds of music, Mr. Page. That's probably why I found Ms. Calloway's observation so interesting. See, I remembered you said the part in question was a soprano solo."

"Don't ask me to remember what she called it."

"Yeah, you mentioned that as well," he noted sheepishly. "Anyway, so I listened to every one of the soprano arias right through until I finally heard it and, sure enough, right at the start of Part Three there's the same melody line. Just like the verse in *Broken Angels*. I mean, when you play the two one after another, it's really a bit uncanny."

"So you're telling me that whoever wrote *Broken Angels* lifted it from Handel?"

"Naw, I doubt it," he replied. "Well not on purpose anyway."

"What do you mean *not on purpose*?"

"Well you gotta remember, in music – western music anyway – there are only 12 notes to choose from, and there are only so many ways you can arrange those notes before some song is going to start sounding like something that came before it. That's just the way it is, whether it's the melody of an aria, or the chord progression for some ole hurtin' tune. Music is all interrelated, Mr. Page, whether somebody wants to admit it or not. After all, what an Ottawa Valley fiddler would call an A-B-A tune, classical music would call Binary Form. Personally I kind of like that. There's something cool about a bunch of weekend warriors like us croonin' out old country favourites that remind somebody like the great Margaret Calloway of a solo she used to sing."

"So you're saying it's not a bad thing."

"I'm saying it's an inevitable thing. And then, when you factor in the role of musical influences …"

"What do you mean 'influences'?"

"Well you have to keep in mind, songwriters and composers don't live in a vacuum. Long before they ever wrote a note they were undoubtedly fans of some style of music or another. So it stands to reason, they'd be a little predisposed to whatever style that was once they got around to the business of writing their own compositions."

"So it's OK for songwriters to borrow from their heroes, is that it? Like maybe the fellah who wrote *Broken Angels* was also a fan of Handel just like you?"

"Maybe he was. Who knows? Mind you I wouldn't use the term *borrow*. That'd be saying it too strongly. I'd just say that certain flavours of music seem to work their way from one generation to the next. Longer than that, I guess, if you consider Ms. Calloway's example. After all Handel's *Messiah* is almost 250 years old. *Broken Angels* was put out in … well let's see … Hey Jake!" He called back over his shoulder toward the guitar player busily changing his strings from his perch on the edge of the stage. "When did

River City release *Broken Angels*? I'm thinking '74 maybe?" He swivelled back to face Murray. "Jake remembers all this stuff," he added.

"Not even close," came the reply. "*Broken Angels* is from their last album, about two-and-a-half years ago. Three years tops."

"Really?"

"And it's not one of theirs," the guitar player went on. "A guy out of Nashville named Drew Stafford wrote it for them. He's the new flavour of the month down there right now ... written a bunch of songs for them and some of the other acts on the Cherry Blossom label."

"You sure about that?" the pedal steel player repeated quizzically. "'Cause if that's the case I'm a bit confused. I mean, I don't want to pry, Mr. Page, but when you asked us to work up that song for your wife's funeral, well I guess I was just under the impression it was something you and she had listened to for a long time."

Murray dropped his head and stared down at his hands. "No," he answered quietly. "Fact is I never heard tell of it till a few weeks before she passed away. See, once Helen got bad, and she couldn't really sit up to read or watch the TV anymore, well, I tried bringing in the radio and we'd listen to the local country station. The music seemed to pick her up a bit so I kept at it. Just so happened the last time we went through all the old photo albums, she was having a pretty good day ... you know, really just thankful for everything good that had happened to us. Well she gave me her last good smile, just as *Broken Angels* came on. There we were ... pictures of us and the kids ... birthdays and camping trips spread out all over the bed ... Helen passed away the next day. It was her letting-go smile, you see."

"Hey Roger, time to go," the guitar player called.

Roger rose to his feet and gave Murray a gentle pat on the shoulder. "Should be three or four songs in, Mr. Page," he said gently, and headed for the stage.

"Oh just one more quick question? If you have a second"

"What's that?"

"Margaret Calloway. Was she really that good?"

The young man paused a moment to organize his reply. "Well Mr. Page, let me put it this way. In a world where you have to be brilliant just to fail … she was the very best."

"But why?"

"What do you mean?"

"Well take that *Messiah* for example. You said it's been going for almost 250 years. So out of all those performances down through the years all over the world, how did she manage to come along and make her version stand out from the rest?"

The musician grinned. "I don't know," he shrugged. "But she did."

■

As promised, the band broke into *Broken Angels* not fifteen minutes later, right on the heels of a short medley of Merle Haggard favourites. But for some reason the words and the music greeted the arena manager's ears differently. For although the testimonial of the song's significance was still fresh on his lips, for the first time since he had made a Saturday afternoon beer a part of his grieving ritual, Murray Page was actually too preoccupied to really listen. Stranger still, he felt no remorse for this, which was fortunate, because with the absence of such guilt came the space for a newer and fresher preoccupation. Murray Page had stumbled across an idea.

He was back the following Saturday, at his usual spot – second table from the front, middle row – but now, thanks to the idea, he was there with a new-found resolve. His eyes were no longer fixed on the empty space before him. They were, instead, busy, focused intently on the pad of paper in front of him and the letter that he had decided he simply must write. To say thank-you to a man he had never met. A man who had shepherded him through such a difficult time – simply by writing such a beautifully sad song. He had come in early so he could solicit the guitar player for some help.

Drew Stafford. He would ask Jake to look up an address for his record company. He would copy out the letter in good that night. Post it Monday morning. And satisfied with the impetus for doing all of this, he also decided – right then and there – he need not return to the Bluewater Tavern again.

Hallelujah

"Shit!" Peter muttered as he scurried out around the café gate and down the sidewalk towards his car. The frustration was in part because his ring had just caught and torn the lining on the pocket of his favourite sportcoat, but also because of the realization that the change he had been so sure he had with him was actually back in his warmer windbreaker, he having opted for something lighter and more stylish at the last moment, given the weather and the occasion. But in his efforts to extricate himself from his wardrobe, he had completely failed to notice the sprawled figure slumped up against the base of the parking meter next to his hatchback until his feet actually made contact with the soles of the man's thoroughly weather-beaten boots.

"Heads up," the figure grunted, freezing the startled young man in his tracks.

"I'm sorry. I didn't notice you there."

"And you weren't really likely to, rushing along the way you were."

"Listen, I'm really in a bit of a hurry right now and, well, at the moment I'm afraid I can't even find any change for myself."

"I don't remember asking for any."

"Well ... whatever then ... Look, I just need to get to the meter, OK?" He switched his search to his pants, finally locating a couple of coins. Two pennies. Shit again!

"Don't worry," the figure sighed. "I'm not lying here trying to stalk you or your boyfriend over there ... or anyone else for that matter. Nevertheless, one of Toronto's finest in uniform informed me I had to move. It seems neither he nor the owner of your little restaurant over there take to someone such as myself gracing the doorstep. Still, I did get a chance to overhear you and your sweetheart from my side of the fence and, by my count, I'd say there are at least three things you need to be straightened out on."

"Listen. I'm not kidding. I really don't have time for–"

"First, St. Cecilia's Day is November 22nd, not the 16th. Second, there's no need for your friend there to consult his program. I can tell you that tonight's soloists are Trevor Messon, Gloria Devereaux, Neil Raynsford and, of course, the incomparable Margaret Calloway."

Peter was momentarily dumbstruck, startled into silence that such a tattered and stained soul could be the source of such information. Furthermore the young man's eyes simply could not resist the grime ground into the seams of the man's parka, the film of filth clouding the lenses of his battered, misshapen glasses, the caked-on flecks of dead skin scaling his cheeks and forehead ... and his hands, reddened with – what was that? Dried blood?

"And third?" he heard himself ask.

"Just this, my friend," the man replied, as he grabbed the base of the parking meter and hoisted himself to his feet. "I'm afraid you're going to find the acoustics in Emerson Place less than ideal tonight."

He pulled out a clear plastic bag full of rolled coins from somewhere beneath his coat. "Here, looks like you could use this," he said, breaking open one of the paper cylinders and tossing a quarter in the young man's direction. "Don't worry ... I still have plenty for where I'm going."

~APRIL 1, 1982~

"This rug has to go," Henry Burgess mumbled to the empty room as he wrestled with the vacuum cleaner, jabbing it under the furniture, dragging it back and forth across the floor in a haphazard attempt to tidy the place before people started to arrive. Not that he was under any illusion that with a few swipes of his second-hand Electrolux he might make his office – or any other part of the Downtown Distress Line Call Centre, for that matter – look like anything more than what it was – a collection of ill-matched furniture gathered from Goodwill stores and yard sales alike, acquired piecemeal and thrown together into a reasonably functional workspace for him and his volunteer staff. Four people during the peak shifts from afternoon until late evening. Three in the mornings. Two overnight. It was a work in progress for sure, but one he was nevertheless proud of, what with all the upgrades over his six years as the Centre's Facilitator. The new desks, though laminated in an unfortunate shade of green, were now at least large enough for the volunteers to spread out case files, agency reference books and the like, while they took their calls. The phones themselves were now all state-of-the-art 1980 models, with call-hold and forwarding options, and the Centre as a whole now boasted three separate lines – still an embarrassment for a city the size of Toronto, he knew – but a far cry from the single telephone that had strained to serve the area when he had first arrived on the job back in '76. And he quite liked the addition of the small barrister lamps which now shone over each of those phones allowing, to his eye at least, proper illumination for the volunteers to fulfill their duties without blasting the room as a whole with cold clinical light. Henry saw this as of particular importance actually, for it was his hope that – despite the limits of his resourcefulness; the budget-stretching; the fundraising, the begging and borrowing – he had still, if only in consolation, created a congenial atmosphere from which his legion of Samaritans could give of themselves, could listen faithfully day in and day out to the hardships of the hopeless and the chronically discouraged. And, strangely, it was the purchase of those lamps that had finally convinced him he had done the trick. Their softened glow simply made the place less of an office and more of a home, especially in the evenings, when like candlelight they reduced the work area to a blanket of friendly shadows. They warmed up the old plaster walls, the filing cabinets that lined those walls, and, of course, his other prized acquisition – one of the two old sofa sectionals he had found at the Sally Ann and immediately positioned right in between those filing cabinets. Plush and cushioned sanctuary for the weary listener in need of a little five-minute respite from shepherding faceless voices through the minefields of their demons.

But the need for sanctuary did not rest solely with his volunteers, which is why that sofa's mate had found its home in the very next room. More and more, Henry Burgess lived his life right there – reviewing call reports, writing and rewriting grant applications, filling out roster schedules, and eventually … hitting the light switch and crashing for the night, or even for just a few hours' rest from his struggle to catch up to the front of a race that, in truth, had no end.

So it was up to the desks and the phones and the lamps … a coffee-maker here, a new bulletin board there … to mark the progress of his tenure. It was at least a comfortable space, he would tell himself whenever he tumbled onto the upholstery, conducive to making almost any meeting go smoothly, be it a negotiation with some social agency representative or a training session to bring new volunteers into the fold. Comfortable enough to begin teaching a room full of well-intentioned recruits the keys to working the phone lines. Teaching them to trust their listening. To resist the urge to instruct. To resist the urge to compare the sheer anguish of some lost soul with something they themselves once fleetingly felt, turning a caller's overwhelming depression into 'a mere subset of yourself', as he liked to put it. To resist uttering the harsh sounds of a '*what you should do*' or an '*If I were you…*' And in the end to understand that through resistance to these urges, there might be healing in the silence. Healing simply by being in the present tense with someone living a completely miserable life, someone with no other audience with whom to share any of that misery.

Those initial training sessions, he believed, still served so well, weeding out the resumé-stuffers, the self-seeking and, frankly, the ones truly troubled themselves, from the role of would-be volunteers. For his opening exercise he would simply have everyone sit around in the comfort of his old friendly sofa, amid the warm glow of his desk lamps, and he would thank one and all for considering the Distress Centre, then require that, going around the room one-by-one, they describe themselves. The only restriction was that no one could resort to self-descriptions that involved a job, a career or schooling. He still couldn't place why the tactic worked so well. He just knew that it did.

There was a knock at the door. Henry snapped from his daydream, quickly checked his watch and switched off the vacuum cleaner, nervously fumbling over the lever and tangling his feet in the serpentine power cord in the process. He was definitely on edge. For tonight's impromptu meeting was no such training session. And judging by the phone calls that had prompted it, Henry was quite certain the evening would not be rescued by any office ambience he may have created. This evening, he was also sure, would test the very tenets that had helped to form the Distress Centre in the first place … long before he had ever taken the job.

"One minute," he called towards the door as he gave up on the task of winding the cord, instead stuffing hose, canister and all in a heap behind a coat tree in the corner of the room. He had been hoping some of his own would arrive first. Irene mostly. His one and only paid staff. Part-time but solid as a rock for the past six years. Or Michelle from Police Services, whom he had invited as another set of ears, though the call hadn't come through her. Even Jason, the volunteer who made the decision to suspend the Distress Centre's tenets in the first place. Or perhaps Andrew himself, assuming Irene had got hold of him.

A second knock. "Damn rug," he mumbled again, kicking down a folded-up corner of the fringe, then hastened to answer the door.

■

Thou shalt break them with a rod of iron
Thou shalt dash them in pieces like a potter's vessel

The moon's light grows dim, filtered and compromised by the sudden onset of cloud bank. Yet he presses on. Though his progress is slowed by the tangle of creaking tree limbs and pine boughs … he presses on, tripping on stump and root, lashed by the whip of unseen saplings bending and recoiling, slipped up by the unsure footing of greasy slush and matted dead leaf in the darkness below.

Thou shalt break them with a rod of iron
Thou shalt dash them in pieces like a potter's vessel

Why do I still stumble, he wonders. Why, when he is no longer of the earth, should such bodily impediments still attack him so? Part of him wants to stop and ponder this, but there is no time. He tries urging himself forward. Faster ... faster than he has yet ever taken this journey. Faster than all those other occasions ... all those mere dress rehearsals.

But then the paradox hits him ... slamming into him anew with the very weight of the now stone-cold sky. *There have been no other attempts.* No succession of events. No sequences, no instances. *No time.* And once again, with his pilgrimage paralyzed, his spirit tumbles into despair, where hope can draw no breath. Once again he opens his mouth to scream for the very first time ... to curse for all eternity his unbreakable hell.

And yet, on this one and only occasion – this singular repetition of torture – that scream fails to arrive, pre-empted by the distant sound of music, still faint, but growing clearer ...

Thou shalt break them ...
Thou shalt break them with a rod of iron

He climbs to his feet and aims for the sound. He has broken through ... just in time. But now he must hurry.

■

Detective Samuels passed the time by tapping a pen against his pad of paper and pacing the room, while he waited for everyone whose presence had been requested to arrive, periodically stopping to sip from the mug of coffee Henry had presented him. Once or twice he tried out one of the three wingback chairs Irene had dragged in from the hallway, before the need to be in motion overtook him once more. Finally, when all were ac-counted for, Henry closed the door leading to the call room, and nodded in the direction of his guest. The detective introduced himself and imme-diately proceeded with the task at hand.

"So you took the call?" he asked, turning to address a tall plump young man in striped track pants and a baseball cap, whom Henry just then remembered from the lad's training loved the Blue Jays and detested the idea of people ordering pineapples on their pizza. ('If God had wanted pineapples on pizza he would have put Italy in the Pacific Ocean,' he remembered the young man joking. Wonderful way to train volunteers, Henry reminded himself.)

"Yes, Sir. Around eight this morning."

"And your name?"

"Jason Canavo."

"But you didn't call us until …" The detective flipped back over an older note. "Until 2:30 this afternoon. Why was that, Jason?"

"Well we hear some pretty offside stuff around here, so I didn't put a whole lot of stock in it 'til I got home from my shift and turned on the news. Then the whole thing just seemed a bit too creepy to be a coincidence, you know?"

"Detective, just for some background, you should know that the Distress Centre has very strict policies on anonymity for both callers and volunteers." The speaker was Michelle Watson from Police Services. "It is only in extraordinary circumstances, when the threat of a public danger seems legitimate, that we normally ask an agency such as this to circumvent these policies."

"No one's asking anyone to circumvent anything," Samuels replied. "We're just here to see if there's anything to connect this caller to the Emerson Place vandalism. So … what can anyone tell me about this fellow, this …" He checked his notes once more, "… Eli?"

"Well he's been phoning us for a number of years," Irene spoke carefully.

"And what's his story?"

Henry stood quickly – though his eyes remained lowered to the floor. "I'm sorry, Detective," he said. "We just can't divulge information like that.

Please be assured we are more than willing to share anything that warrants your attention with regard to your investigation, but to open Eli's or any other caller's whole file would be a serious breach of the Distress Centre's Protocols. Protocols," he added quickly, just as the detective's arms flopped to his sides, "that must be strictly adhered to and regulated, as they are explicit conditions for many of the government grants and foundation bursaries we receive to operate this agency. That said, I can confirm that the man in question, Eli, is a regular caller and that during his conversations he has shown a particular interest in the architecture and the construction of Emerson Place."

"That's right. I've talked to him lots of times," Jason piped in again, with more eagerness than the facilitator would have liked.

"Define 'lots'," the detective inquired.

"Maybe ten or fifteen times over the two years I've been here. He gets foul in the mouth from time to time. I mean, he's got a real temper, for sure. But he was always an OK call. I figure he's just one of those people who needs to get stuff off his chest. You know, a lot to say but nobody to say it to. So by the time he dials us up he's already pretty riled up."

Irene dropped the forearm that had been holding up her weary head. "But Jason, if you are aware how Eli can get, why didn't you just come to us first?"

"No, Irene. I'm sorry. You weren't there. He was completely different this time. I mean, he's snapped."

"And would that still be your opinion if you hadn't turned on the news this afternoon?" the assistant countered.

"Kind of a moot point now, isn't it?" the detective cut in. "What was he saying, Son?" Samuels stepped towards the volunteer causing Jason, through a sudden involuntary flexing of his shoulder and locking of his knees, finally to appreciate the squeeze of his predicament. Quickly he looked toward Henry who, in turn, glanced over at Irene. Her return shrug allowed an eventual nod from the facilitator.

"OK," Jason began with a sigh of relief. "He was saying, 'I did it! I did it!' Over and over. And so I asked him what it was he did. Then he was just swearing and mumbling 'Fucking Emerson Place ... goddamn place'. And I commented that tonight was opening night. And that's when he came back with 'Just might be closing night for some!' So I ask him again what he means and that's when he started laughing with this really creepy voice that just wasn't like anything I ever heard from him before. And then he says ... and I'm sorry, I'm just quoting here ... he says, 'Keep out the fucking Jews. Once and for all, keep out the goddamn fucking Jews!' Like I said, the guy always sounded like he had problems, but I never heard him come anywhere close to anything like that before."

"But he did speak ill of Emerson Place on previous occasions, correct?"

Irene nodded slowly. "Since they first announced the construction of the place, Eli has spoken about the building's design with a fair degree of sophistication," she explained.

"And aside from this morning, that's been the focus of his phone calls?"

Jason and Irene looked to one another and nodded in agreement.

"You're absolutely sure?"

"Yes," Henry reiterated.

"Yes," from Irene.

"No," came a third reply and all in the room spun toward the sound of the dissenting voice coming from behind the door that separated the meeting from the duties of the call attendants. Presently the fair hair and droopy posture of a slightly uncertain-looking man possibly in his late twenties or early thirties edged into the room. "Well, not for me anyway," he amended cautiously, his eyes, like Jason's before him, also appealing towards Henry for assurance before proceeding any further.

"Andrew, are you on shift this evening?"

The young man nodded and pointed back behind him "Frank called me earlier and asked if I could fill in. I already have the overnight shift but he's really down with the flu, so I came in after work. Sorry to interrupt, but I couldn't help overhearing."

"Not a problem. We were actually trying to track you down. Everyone, this is Andrew. He's been a volunteer at the Centre for many years. I believe from even before my time here, isn't that right, Andrew?"

"I started right after college back in the spring of '74," the young man replied.

"Detective Samuels, I think it's worth noting that Andrew's call reports paint a much more moderate picture of Eli. Andrew, since you're between calls in there, I'm wondering if you could expand on this for us?" Henry stood up and slid his desk chair over to the lad who, with another nod, lowered himself slowly, rubbing his palms together as he decided how to begin.

"Well I've only been on the phone with Eli three or four times."

"Just tell us what you know," the detective urged, checking his watch.

"Well the very first time I talked to him … and I swear to God, Henry, I don't know why … he called me by name."

"That's right!" Jason blurted out again. "He always used to start his calls like that. 'Where's Andrew? I want to talk to Andrew!'"

"Andrew 03," Irene amended. "He'd always ask for Andrew 03."

"Wait a minute! Wait a minute!" The detective interjected in a manner that, along with his sidelong squint and scrunched nostril, let everyone in the room know he was quickly growing dissatisfied with the pace of things. "Mr. Burgess."

"Henry."

"You mean to tell me after your whole song and dance about anonymity, both on the phone this afternoon and now here again as I try to conduct what I will remind you all is a very time-sensitive investigation …" He waved his notepad in the direction of Andrew, causing the young man to straighten his posture. "You mean to tell me these people who call in here know the identity of who they're talking to?"

There was a pause that fell short of mutual disdain, though not by a great margin, before Irene cleared her throat and, noticing the still-averted eyes of her boss, decided to take the initiative herself.

"Officer Samuels."

"Detective."

"Detective, then," she repeated with a squinting smile. "The downside to running a Distress Call Centre such as this one, is that it is not foolproof from those who choose to prey on the truly legitimate service it provides. The vast majority of our calls come from sincerely desperate people needing to talk out a situation – depression, thoughts of suicide, abusive spouses, substance problems, gangs … the whole gamut. But to keep ourselves available to those callers, we have to endure those who prey. The guy who wants to hear a female voice so he can masturbate to the sound of companionship. The bully who wants to inflict verbal harm on someone … anyone. And yes, this includes those who are truly disturbed yet resourceful … the caller who can simulate a troubled soul and call time and again, keeping journals on whom they spoke to and what personal details that person might have let slip during their duty as a friendly voice on the line."

"But Eli wasn't like that," Andrew spoke up, again – much like his first comment from the next room, seemingly in spite of himself. "You see, I really don't mind using my first name talking to people. I know some of the volunteers choose to use an alias. Personally I don't feel the need. And sure, I was a little dumbfounded that first time, what with the guy blurting out my name right off the top, telling me he's been calling and calling, just waiting to talk to me. I mean that would put up anybody's guard. But after a few seconds of chatting, it was pretty clear I wasn't the person he thought I was."

"And further to that point," Irene added, "as a matter of record, Detective, you should know that Eli has been calling us and requesting to speak to someone named Andrew for a number of years.

"And what about this 03 you mentioned earlier?" Samuels inquired. "What's the significance of that?"

Irene and Henry shrugged in tandem. "Not a clue," she replied. "Something he got in his head, I guess."

Henry cleared his throat and reached for the top of a large stack of files teetering precariously on the edge of his desk. "I took the liberty of pulling some of the notes you made from those calls, Andrew. That's another thing, Detective. We ask all our volunteers to write a brief summary on all the calls they take. And without going into specifics …"

"No … couldn't have that," the detective mumbled to himself.

"… the thing I noticed immediately about these reports is that Andrew made no reference to the topics that all the other volunteers all state so prominently. No mention of architecture or classical music, which by the way, he also discusses at length. Certainly nothing about Emerson Place."

"But that's all the guy *ever* talks about," Jason reiterated, turning to face his fellow volunteer.

"Sorry," Andrew shrugged. "Never came up."

"There's also nothing about how angry he seemed on the phone."

Another shrug.

"Well, suppose we speed things up a bit and you tell me how he *did* seem," Samuels cut in, checking the time again.

"Well … sad, mostly. Really sad in fact. Too sad to really be able to tell me the cause or the root of it all, you know?"

"Would he ask details about you? Give you any clues about who he thought you were?"

The young man shook his head as he tried to remember. "I don't think so. Did I write anything about that?"

Henry skimmed the file notes but he too ended up merely shaking his head.

"I mean at the start of that first call he did seem genuinely happy to be talking to me. Or at least, the me he thought I was. But even that was only to a point."

"What do you mean?"

"Well as I recall, even before I was sure I had convinced him I wasn't who he was looking for, it was like this curtain of depression had already fallen down on him. I remember thinking – I think I wrote this down, Henry – that maybe finding the actual Andrew he was looking for would be sadder than not finding him, if that makes any sense."

"So would you say he was delusional?" Samuels continued, head down, as he scratched notes into his pad.

"What? No ... well, maybe. I mean what do I know? I'm no psychiatrist or anything. He did seem to bounce around a lot."

"Bounce around how?"

"With the here and now. Sometimes he'd speak like we were long-lost pals. Like he was going to ask me to go fishing with him or something."

"Fishing?" The detective paused his pen.

"Hypothetically speaking ... oh, and one time he started talking like I was a little kid ... an infant even. He actually started singing to me. And of course, since he was so depressed, he cried a lot. He cried a lot that particular call, come to think of it."

"Anything else," the detective urged.

"Don't think so ... well, he was pretty hard to get off the line, but you could say that about most of our regular callers."

"Would you say he was capable of hurting or injuring someone?"

"What?"

"Out of anger ... or depression ..."

"What? No ... why? What's happened?" the young man asked, scanning every face in the room but receiving only worried glances in return.

"*Has* he hurt someone?"

Again silence, while everyone in the room waited for the detective to finish up his notation. "Not yet," he mumbled, and with one final glance at his watch, and only the briefest of nods in Henry's direction, saw himself out the door.

~DECEMBER 11, 2010~

Thou shalt break them with a rod of iron ...

For a moment her writhing subsides and her mind flies back to her days on the stage, awaiting her turn while Neil sang that wonderful aria. *Thou shalt dash them in pieces ...* delivering its rich phrasing with such muscle ... the perfect foil for the upcoming –

The recollection abandons her unfinished, her brief blissful respite overcome by the sudden realization of what was to follow. Her eyes pop open, her fingernails dig and paw for the armrests once more. "No," she grunts, quite audibly, and her gaze meets the disapproving steel-blue eyes of the woman next to her, who – despite her glaring, Maggie decides – looks quite fetching in her short blunt hairdo. "Almost at the Hallelujah," the woman leans in and hisses, though the notice, rather than placating Maggie, only causes her to fight and strain all the more.

"Damn it, Mother ... it's OK. Everything's OK," she hears the woman mutter, though she cannot agree. Not at all. How can any of this be OK? When there's so little time, she thinks, though as soon as the thought greets her, she realizes she cannot specify time for what. To prepare? To brace herself to remember? No, anything but that, she realizes, and begins her writhing anew. She is desperate for diversion. Desperate to cast her mind in any other direction. Anywhere else but there, with that chorus ... that damned chorus – the last music she ever sang before the fall of her career – ringing forever in her ears.

For Christ's sake, you old hag, she berates herself, you sang for forty years. Where are your memories? What about Carnegie ... yes, Carnegie ... the time you wore the pale green gown with the ruffle. Oh the fuss they made over you! And the reception afterwards, in the Oak Room at the Algonquin no less!

"Mother!" the woman hisses again, and in her mind Maggie agrees ... yes, just the type of fuss Mother would have wanted! And then there was the review in *The Times* the next day. Probably the finest since the BBC recording years before, perhaps even more glowing, the way they lauded your interpretation unconditionally. "*I'm sorry, Miss Calloway. Have we switched places? Have my years of interpretation been trumped so completely by the young farm girl from Ontario?*"

"Shut up!" She blurts out, sending necks craning and heads spinning from two rows before and aft, heads trying to identify the disruptive sobs – the tortured mantra of "Not now, not now" interrupting the final phrases of the aria on stage.

The woman lunges for her, almost climbing into her chair. She must be trying to help me, Maggie reasons, from the way she takes my head and cradles my jaw. Yes, she wants to help you Maggie. She wants to help free your hands. Get you out of here before it's too late! "Yes help me ... help me forget all of this!" she wants to say, but the words are muzzled by the woman's hand; indeed they are drowned by the downstroke of the violins leading the charge into the chorus. NO! Remember something else, goddamn it. Christ, all those other concerts! *Acis and Galatea*, the Brahms Requiem. Hell, all those years of recitals and chamber series. Anything but this!

How she longs for a Jameson. A whole goddamn bottle too ... to douse the relentless hell of her own private legacy! Yes, she dreams, some Jameson in some hidden out-of-the-way bar with old wooden tables and chairs. She is struck by the idea. Is it fantasy or memory? Did she simply conjure up the notion? And if so, who is that she sees herself chatting with? But the image is too fleeting, overwhelmed by the vibrant onslaught of strings striking down on Handel's most famous of four-note motifs ...

... once ... then again ...

~APRIL 1, 1982~

"Good night, Henry," Irene called back over her shoulder as she folded her coat on her arm and headed for the door. She'd rinse the mugs in the morning; leave Eli's files for then too. Given the way her boss still had them fanned out across his desk she knew well enough he was going to spend a good deal more of the evening mulling them over.

"But just one thing," she paused to add, her hand already poised on the doorknob, for in truth she was of equal mind to leave her curiosity for the morning as well. "Seeing as everyone's gone, can you tell me if you believe there's anything more to this than a cop's over-excitement?"

Henry stared at the collage of notes from Eli's phone conversations and shrugged. "I've investigated a few of his calls in the past, when the volunteers have complained."

"But really, Henry," she sighed, turning back to face him. "How many of our regulars could we say that about?"

"I know, I know."

"And nine times out of ten – hell, ninety-nine times out of a hundred – it turns out to be some shut-in who's too scared to step out their door let alone hurt somebody ... let alone blow up a theatre, or whatever the hell that detective thinks Eli is capable of. I mean, as far as we know he's still at the Institute, isn't he?"

"Off and on. That much I know. Like I said I've made a few inquiries in the past." He broke off his self-induced trance and leaned forward in his chair to grab a small stack of papers that he had previously separated from the bulk of the files. "I skimmed through these before the meeting. Back a few months ago, one of our volunteers named … let's see … Bunnie?"

"That's Bonnie."

"What? Oh right … impossible handwriting," he noted with a squint towards the page. "Anyway, Bonnie filed a complaint that stated she didn't appreciate being yelled and sworn at by an anti-Semite."

"Well that's the other thing about Jason's account of anti-Jewish ha-tred. I mean, wouldn't you think someone named Eli might himself be–"

"Yes, you'd think, wouldn't you? But Bonnie said she made the mistake of offering the opinion that anti-Jewish sentiment was no longer a prob-lem in this day and age."

"There's her first problem … offering opinions."

"Yes, well … from the notes she made of the call it sounds like Eli got after her pretty hard. According to this, he said, 'You don't see anti-Jewish? Hell, I still got lots of anti-Jewish!' Then according to Miss Penmanship here, he went on a bit of a rant about … let's see … the 'Furking Kites.'"

"Henry, come on!"

"I'm sorry. I'm just tired," he sighed, tossing the report down in favour of the next in the stack. "This is another one. Similar complaint."

"More anti-Semitism?"

"No … this time it was abortion, by the looks of it here," he relayed, scanning through the write-up, checking the top of the page for a filing date. "It's from quite a while back, too. But the volunteer wrote that Eli was fit to be tied."

"So we have an anti-Semitic right-to-lifer."

"And of course there are all these others about Emerson Place," he noted, thumb-fanning the remaining reports through the palm of his hand.

Irene turned again for the exit. "Anti-Semitic, right-to-lifer, anti-patron of the arts ..."

"Equals?"

"Equals harmless shut-in. Dollars to donuts," she concluded.

"Maybe ... and then again maybe Eli's the one out of a hundred who goes against form. Then where are we?"

Irene paused a moment, compelled by a number of possible responses. Like informing her boss that he worked too hard. That he took matters too much to heart. Stayed far too late too many nights. But then, as was always the case when these notions struck her, she deferred to silence, save for her cursory little sigh of exasperation – far too subtle ever to catch the man's single-minded attention – and with one more "'Night Henry" over her shoulder she crossed the threshold, back into the world at large.

"Oh, Irene?" Henry called after her.

"Mmm?"

"What do *you* make of Eli's Andrew 03 reference, anyway?"

"Don't know," she returned from the other side of the door. "See you tomorrow, Henry."

"I mean as long as I've been here none of our volunteers go by a number alongside their name."

The sound of the outer door closing was the only reply.

"I don't think I'd even allow something like that," the facilitator continued mumbling to himself. "I mean that's the point of anonymity; if there are seven Andrews or Berts or Mary-Anns in here, a caller gets whichever one picks up. Why assign a specific number to differentiate yourself from the others? It's for the volunteer's own safety–"

His voice trailed away, faded not by the realization he no longer had an audience, but by the weight of a far different notion, hatched from the opening words of his own little soliloquy. "*As long as I've been here,*" Henry mouthed again, letting the phrase work on him a moment. Then, in an instant he was off, grabbing for his key chain, and heading for the basement where distant files of decades past – for distressed callers and volunteers alike – resided in a forgotten little storage room behind the old building's boiler. Quickly he descended, two stairs at a time, muttering a slight prayer that the files in question would still be correlated or alphabetized or categorized in some logical manner. He fumbled for the correct key, oblivious to the oppressive heat that the furnace was throwing in the close confines. It was after all really nothing more than an oversized closet. Once it was unlocked, he pawed blindly at the door frame and the walls, searching for any evidence of a light switch, until his forehead made startling contact with a long feathery strand of something, which he rather spastically batted at, then caught, then pulled on. And there by the light of a single forty-watt bulb, Henry Burgess found what he was looking for; a file with but one faded report regarding an otherwise forgotten volunteer. On its tab, just as the facilitator had expected, was the heading *Andrew 03*. But in brackets below, which he had not at all foreseen … a second name.

Eli Benowitz.

■

"You're gay, aren't you?" the old man stated loudly and deliberately, and with a distinctly disconcerting grin watched his pronouncement take its effect on the young man's rigid back and tightened shoulder muscles. "Now don't get upset. It's not like you were hiding it, staring into your boyfriend's eyes with that look on your face. Too bad he wasn't returning the favour, though. I would imagine that is somewhat bothersome for you."

"He's just a little more reserved, that's all." Peter heard himself respond and instantly felt disgusted for being goaded into a character defence to a complete stranger.

"Are you sure about that? Maybe he's reserved because he's not quite as proud to be out here in the open as you are."

"And maybe this is none of your business," the young man returned, spinning around and striking out down the sidewalk, back towards the café, conscious of his effort to maintain an unaffected air ... if not for the old man, then at least for Kyle, should he happen to be looking. Sadly, however, he was unable to resist the urge to sneak a glimpse back at the man.

It was that demonstration of nervousness that surely signalled his weakness. The stranger came right after him, following close behind his shoulder. "In fact, maybe he's ashamed. Maybe what you see as reserved is just his inability to tell you that!"

Peter quickened his pace. God, how he hated confrontation. How he wished Kyle was there with him. Kyle was far more equipped to handle unsolicited taunting like this. Would know just the right disarming thing to say and how to say it. Peter glanced back again. He was still there ... now grinning even more ... and moving up even with the young man's elbow.

"Maybe he'd rather your little affair just run its course and die of its own causes than spare himself the discomfort of telling you the truth, ah?"

"Not interested," Peter replied, throwing up his palms and again quickening his gait as he attempted to step out and around the man's shoulder. But the old man spun ahead himself and blocked the lad in his tracks.

"Not interested, he says ... not interested!" the man mocked, backing Peter towards the fence that bordered the café, the leading edge of his odour – the stagnant stench of dried spit and mucous hanging from his chin and beard – proving force enough on its own to pin him there.

"Tell me, my friend," he challenged, "are you really so simple as to think you guys have cornered the market on discrimination? Sitting over there in the sunshine with everyone just leaving you be. Never once thinking about the backs of the generations that came before you ... the backs you're standing on right now just so you can hold hands and lift your chin up and still feel all that sunshine. And look at you now! One little confrontation from some tired old fucker and you just cower away all timid and scared."

"Excuse me?" Peter finally retaliated. "You think this is easy for us? You think it doesn't take courage?"

The old man moved in closer. Too close for the young man to fixate on anything other than rotted yellow teeth, the deposits of foam gathered in the corner of his mouth, the crusty residue caked on the whiskers below his nose, the eyeglasses teetering low on that nose. And the smell. The suffocating smell that now, even more than the sight of the man, caused him to throw his head sideways and squint off water-eyed into the distance.

"What I think ... is that there's one big fucking difference!" he spat back contemptuously and through all-but-closed eyes Peter saw a grimy right hand come flying up from below his line of sight. Instinctively the young man grimaced, bracing himself to accept the angry blow. But the contact that followed proved nothing more than a gentle palm cupped around his cheek. "You two lovebirds still have the promise of a someday ... when none of this bullshit matters anymore."

Slowly Peter opened his eyes and for an undeniable split second – he was sure he had not 'romanticized' it, as Kyle would say – he smelled nothing, was revolted by nothing, indeed saw nothing ... but a man. He looked so sad. Just in that instant of locked eyes ... so undeniably sad. Peter wanted to say something ... tried to say something. But his words were beaten by those of the stranger. The old man leaned in and with his cheek now pressed firmly against the young man's face whispered in his ear. "You lucky bastards."

Then he was off across the street, with nothing more to offer, save for the one-fingered salute to the onlooking café.

■

"Ashby Psychiatric Institute, Night Desk. This is Carol Heath. How can I help you?"

"Carol, I'm glad it's you. It's Henry Burgess over at the Distress Centre."

"Well Henry, imagine my surprise."

"I'm sorry?"

"A very nice detective was just here visiting me–"

"Samuels."

"He says you weren't much help in trying to get information on a suspect of his."

"Eli Benowitz."

"Not to worry," she chuckled. "I have no doubt he's saying the very same thing about me right about now. You know I don't expect every cop to respect or even understand the system, but you'd think with a detective who's been around the block I wouldn't have to waste my entire dinner break regurgitating the tenets of doctor/patient confidentiality."

"I'm sorry to hear that."

"Comes with the territory."

"No, I mean I'm sorry because I'm afraid I may have you repeating those same tenets all over again."

"Oh God. Not you too?"

"Listen, Carol, do you have Eli's case file handy?"

"Henry, please."

"Not diagnoses or medical history. Nothing confidential. I just need some facts about him. Age, place of birth. Where he's lived."

There was something slightly encouraging in the sigh from the other end of the phone. "OK ... just a minute ... Eli ... Eli ... OK. No birth date given. Born in Europe ... doesn't say where ..."

"Religious affiliation?"

"Jewish. But it looks like it's been scratched out."

"Really? Listen, Carol. Are you by any chance reading from something Eli would have filled out himself?"

"Grey area, Mr. Burgess."

"Sorry ... sorry. Anything else that's not so grey then?"

"Not much, I'm afraid. He was a foster child in a family that immigrated to Canada in 1946. I can tell you that. It would explain the sketchy birth record. What else? Let's see ... He went to university here in Toronto. His mother died in 1960. His father in 1964. Says that he moved to England for quite a while after that."

"England?"

"Found work on quite a few construction projects in and around London."

"That would make sense."

"If you say so. It mentions working on renovations to a couple of hospitals. Reconstruction of a Hall of Records in some place called Shoreditch.

A children's services registry, also in Shoreditch … a theatre. You know this really is bending the limits, Henry."

"Did you say a theatre?"

"Yes, that one seemed to interest the detective as well."

"Can you tell me when he moved back to Canada?"

"1974."

"And he wouldn't have known a soul, in all likelihood."

"What's that?"

"Nothing … just talking to myself. Carol, when was he first admitted to Ashby?"

"Sorry, Hombre … this is a current file. Can't go there."

"OK, OK … sorry again," Henry relented, tapping his pen on the newly-found file in front of him, its silver tip and band glistening beneath the beam of his desk lamp, flashing flecks of light in front of his absent stare as he searched for some different tack.

"I've got it!" he exclaimed without warning. "Carol?"

"Still here," the nurse sighed. "On my dinner break …"

"I have an idea."

"Henry, really, like I told your detective friend–"

"No, Carol. Listen up. I want to read you a report from one of our old records I just found in storage. Now, if the details don't agree with your files on Eli then I swear you can lecture me about the tenets of doctor/patient confidentiality for the rest of the night."

"That's sweet, Henry, but believe it or not I actually have more important things to do."

"But if it does match … I mean even a bit … then I want you to just hang up. OK?" And without even waiting for the woman's compliance, he charged ahead.

~DECEMBER 11, 2010~

It's too late. They're all standing up … choir and audience alike. Just like the King of England did, she reminds herself; he stood right up for the Hallelujah on that very first London concert all those years ago, though try as she might she cannot recall the reason why.

Another voice whispers in her ear, "Come on, Maggie. It's *Hallelujah time.*" And she feels a gentle hand – gentler than the last lady's – sliding under her armpit, another pressed against her spine to straighten up her posture. *A soloist should always exude poise throughout the enterprise of any vocal delivery*, she reminds herself, and in doing so suddenly remembers. It's deference. People rise for the Hallelujah Chorus out of deference. Instinctively her hands move to find and smooth the fabric of her gown before she rises … the pale green with the ruffle. But really, they needn't make such a fuss, she thinks, lifting her busy hands from her hem to acknowledge the audience left and right.

"Damn it, Mother, no!" comes a second voice; curt and desperate. Not at all *poised.* And with it, yet another arm, this one squeezing tightly and pulling on her clothing. "Get up. It's the Hallelujah."

Ah yes, the Hallelujah she is reminded. Where soloists and choir sing as one. Always such a lovely touch, she thinks, then begins the task of focusing as she prepares for the first soprano entry. Yes, forget the haven of memories. Forget the cover of fantasy. She will conquer her demons with the only tool that had ever proved powerful enough to distract her from her self.

Slowly she draws for deep and even breath, rehearses in her mind the placement of that opening note, high up in the arching chamber of her mouth, focuses on the resonance she is about to impart. She is ready. She is eager. So eager, in fact, her voice precedes the first collective intake of breath from 200 voices strong … the sound croaking from her tired sagging breast, only briefly heard by the few rows around her before being swallowed up by the choir.

Rest your weary heart
My broken little angel …

The face jumps for her again. Such a beautifully serious face, she thinks. Then the hand – the one that had been pulling on her fine pale green gown no less – is back over her mouth. Another set of hands is on her back. Rows of heads are rising up, rising up like music towards the dome ceiling above. Further and further towards its bright blue smoothness, its ornate golden trim. What a beautiful building, she thinks to herself as she falls … what a beautiful, beautiful building …

Chorus:
Worthy is the Lamb …

Tonight Emerson Place is thrilled to have world-renowned soprano and Ontario native Margaret Calloway christen our stage. For over three decades Ms. Calloway has enjoyed an illustrious solo career both in concert and in the recording studio, most recently with her tour of the Far East with the Melbourne Philharmonic Orchestra in the fall of 1980, and with the critical acclaim of her latest album, a recital of Ralph Vaughn Williams songs, released under the Valmont label in the fall of 1981.

Ms. Calloway began her career studying under Dr. Enid Blaisdell at Toronto's St. Timothy's College before moving quickly to the prestigious Lincolnshire Voice Academy in England, where she gained instant acclaim for her clarity of tone and enigmatic interpretation of phrasing. Indeed, it was the seminal 1951 BBC recording of the Academy's Concert Series that laid the foundation for the singer's long-standing love affair with Handel's *Messiah*. Of that performance itself, the esteemed *London Times* critic Nigel Lindsay wrote, "Surely new life was breathed into an old classic tonight. Ms. Calloway shone; her voice an intoxicating blend of ingénue and maturity." And as Dame Helen Smithfield noted in her review of the recording of said concert, "In particular the beloved *I Know That My Redeemer Liveth* is delivered with a humanity that has hitherto been undiscovered in the libretto. Her interpretation, so heartfelt, so personalized, sung almost as a question rather than a statement, transcends perhaps even the most lofty expectations of Handel himself. Beguiling, complex in its nuance and shading, it is as the Mona Lisa's smile and I, for one, count myself the better for the privilege of listening."

Welcome home, Ms. Calloway.

~APRIL 1, 1982~

The theatre manager led Detective Samuels back stage through a laby-
rinth of corridors and dressing rooms teeming with choristers and musicians, some leafing through music as they either mouthed or fingered a few
of the trickier upcoming passages, others more concerned with straighten-
ing ties and adjusting straps, teasing and spraying hair. He stretched his
neck over the sea of heads, trying to get a sense of the place as it might
have looked for the perpetrator the night before, for while the detective
had investigated countless vandalisms throughout his career, he could not
recall many cases of defacing property that would have required such pre-
meditation. After all, this vandal had not merely happened upon an irre-
sistibly accessible target. He would have had to research, plan and time out
the act to a considerably high degree of detail, especially given the fact he
had accomplished the deed right under the noses of all the manpower that
would have been scrambling to put the finishing touches on the place in
time for this evening's opening. And then again, he reasoned, perhaps that
was the plan's genius. Such a hectic workspace could see so many painters,
electricians, delivery people, carpenters all so busy running this way and
that, they would have little or no inclination to question the presence of
one more body. What better time to slip in a side door and simply bide
one's time.

His mind flashed back to his very first case, a ring up in Orillia that
was stealing building supplies out along the cottage roads. How they just
pulled up in a truck with a contractor's business name painted on the side,
and the rest was easy. No one driving by would even question the sight of
such a vehicle, let alone stop to inquire whether the man wrestling with the
stacks of drywall and lumber was actually delivering them to the job site
or helping himself to materials already there. He recalled the collar – the
first of his career no less – the guilty party caught red-handed straddling a
pack of shingles intended for a large A-frame cottage (the very design that

gave the detective the idea for renovating his father's property at Bala a few years later).

A tap on the shoulder brought the detective back to the evening at hand.

"You'll find Ms. Calloway in the last dressing room on your left," the theatre manager stated and pointed, planting her feet and hugging her clipboard in a fashion that let Samuels know in no uncertain terms that she had no intention of escorting him any further. With a light nod of gratitude the detective set off down the corridor alone, curious to learn what – if anything – would be the reaction of this seemingly formidable woman to his news of the crime. Distress? Outrage? Disinterest, more than likely, he surmised, reminding himself once again – yes, like that annoying phone line facilitator had gone on about – that even explicit hate-crime messages such as this one were rarely anything more than their own ends. The goal rather than the means. 'The bomb scares of the artistic world', he remembered an old desk sergeant once describe them. Perpetrated by those only brave enough to put a scare into folks when they're sure no one else is looking. Samuels wanted to believe that was the case here. If only there hadn't been the one specific reference …

He had managed to save it from the press. Also noted that it wasn't a part of Jason the volunteer's story either. Nevertheless, there it had been, scrawled only once mind you – like an afterthought, or perhaps some-thing that took working up to. They had found it just inside the front mez-zanine entrance on the right-hand side of the hall. The words that con-nected her to the crime. The words that referenced her so specifically … so ungraciously.

No, something was definitely amiss. He was sure. Hell, why else would that same facilitator have finally got off his high horse and called him back, not two hours after their meeting. It was a detail that in retrospect, during the detective's writing and filing of the case report, would remain a point of irritation. For after enduring all the man's platitudes about privileged information and caller privacy … not two hours later, there's his message blinking away on Samuels' machine … Henry Burgess from down at the Distress Centre, claiming he *just happened* to dig up some further details about the caller in question.

Further details my ass, the detective scoffed, and knocked on the dressing room door.

■

Volunteer File #317
Name: Eli Benowitz
Volunteer Nickname: Andrew 03

Service Start Date: March 14, 1974
Services terminated: May 8, 1974

NOTES:

Volunteer in question has been removed from active roster as of May 8, 1974 for continued erratic behaviour during call sessions. Volunteer was observed on two separate occasions answering "phantom" calls when there was no party on the line. During the second of these two reported instances, volunteer was found "conversing" with an imaginary caller whom he referred to by his own Distress Centre call name, Andrew 03.

Three other situations were documented citing incidents where the volunteer was found shouting obscenities at callers, and being belligerent and confrontational with fellow volunteers. The most significant of these incidents included threats of "I will hunt you down. I can find you" to a female caller whom, according to fellow volunteer testimony, he believed to be someone from his past. Pursuant to this testimony, the volunteer in question was relieved of his services immediately and, as per

Distress Centre protocols, authorities were notified.

FOLLOW-UP ACTION: Not known

∎

~DECEMBER 11, 2010~

There's a commotion somewhere. Somewhere overhead, off to the side in the grey beyond her view. It's a sound of uncertainty … of music stopping haphazardly, lost instruments and voices gradually abandoning their phrases one by one. Like a dying wave falling on shore, she thinks. Or a cloud passing over the sun. She hears it first with the tenors, then as it makes its way through the choir as a whole. Then the strings, starting with the cellos nearest her …

It's because of that bloody commotion no doubt, she concludes. But what exactly is going on? She strains to see but there are too many heads in the way – gawking anxious heads all huddled in and murmuring away about something – their dull drone gradually filling the void left by the now-subsided score. It's their fault, she thinks. They're to blame, talking amongst themselves so loudly … so loudly, why they have brought the music to a complete halt.

A woman emerges from the crowd of them. A frantic woman. Crazed. Screaming. She squints to make out the woman's face but it's too difficult to see. Too difficult because they're dimming the lights now. Off and on. Off and on. Slightly dimmer with each flicker. Perhaps they're ready to continue the concert, she reasons. Perhaps they're ready to finish. And yet the screaming woman persists. She doesn't want this to happen. She wants them all to stop. She's screaming for everyone to stop …

~APRIL 1, 1982~

The knock on her dressing room door could not have come at a more inopportune time, there in the midst of her intermission routine – the same requisite scales and arpeggiated sequences that had served her so well for over three decades, completely automatic, completely rote, yet still as absolutely necessary as the first time she ever performed.

"Get in here if it's that important!" she called over her shoulder, though only after her first reply of "I'm busy" had been answered in turn by more and louder knocking. The door opened and she shrugged impatiently toward the tall robust figure reflected in her makeup mirror.

"Well?"

"Ms. Calloway, I'm Detective Samuels with Metro Toronto Police."

"Yes, I know. And I distinctly remember telling the stage manager your matter would have to wait. You do realize I have a concert to get back to in ten minutes?"

"Yes, Ma'am, I'm aware of that. But time is truly of the essence."

"Then I trust you'll at least be as brief as possible," she proclaimed with a willful stare as the detective stepped inside the dressing room and closed the door behind him. She studied the man's demeanour as he ever so slowly pulled pen and pad from a pocket inside his coat, trying to decide if his deliberate actions were not just some sort of display, an unspoken attempt to trump her agenda with his own.

"I assume this has something to do with the vandalism last night," she sighed and grabbed a liner pencil, applying some reinforcement below her lashes. "It's all anybody was talking about around here this afternoon. But

I can assure you, Detective, neither I nor any of the other soloists would have seen a thing, since we didn't arrive until well past two o'clock, long after the crews had had the whole place painted over again. Which, I might add, is exactly what I already told the officers at the time. And by the way, you've nine minutes now."

"I'm afraid there's more to it than that, Ma'am," Samuels returned, head still down, writing God-knows-what, for clearly she hadn't said anything of any consequence. "You see, while we were investigating the incident we came across a connection between the person we suspect responsible for the crime and yourself."

"Me?" She snorted a laugh that the detective would never have associated with a performer of classical music. "A connection? Me and some anti-Semite with a can of paint?"

The detective finally looked up. "Given some subsequent new information about the man, we're now not sure it was merely a hate crime per se, Ma'am."

Maggie turned from her mirror to face him directly. "Really," she replied. "And since when does KEEP OUT THE FUCKING JEWS sprayed across a public building fail to constitute a hate crime?"

"Well the new information suggests that it was perhaps meant to be more of a testimony ..."

"A testimony?" The soloist tossed her makeup back to the counter and threw up her hands. "Detective, I don't doubt you feel there's some grounds for waltzing in here and discussing the motive of some vandal. But really ... I'm fine. The other soloists are fine. It was an awful thing that happened, but now it's business as usual. And since I now have only ..." She glanced up at the clock above the mirror, "...seven minutes to prepare for the rest of this concert–"

"There was something else on the wall," the detective cut her off with an air of authority she had not anticipated, one that more than matched her own. "It was down towards the front of the hall ..."

"And ..."

"Ma'am, please know I've been doing this for twenty-three years and I would not intrude like this if the situation did not warrant it. Now, I have managed to shield this matter from the press, the theatre staff, even most of the uniformed officers ... at least until we had a better idea of–"

"Oh Detective, for Christ's sake. Just tell me what was on the goddamn wall."

"*Maggie Calloway says keep out the Fucking Jew.*"

The soloist's jaw dropped open.

"We no longer believe Emerson Place or the Jewish community is actually his target, Ma'am." the detective pressed on. "We think you are, Ma'am."

"Because he painted a sign saying I hate the Jews? I don't hate the Jews–"

"No, Ma'am, he didn't say *Jews* in this instance," the detective explained. "He said *Jew*, and we believe the Jew in question may actually be himself."

Had his eyes been on her and not back scanning the evening's hastily-jotted notes, he would have seen – even before he got around to asking her if she recognized the name Eli Benowitz – that this bit of news had hit her like a detonated bomb, ripping apart like shrapnel the veneer of her well-acclaimed life in but a fraction of a second.

She felt faint. Faint and unsteady. "Ms. Calloway ... Ma'am, are you alright?" the detective called out, finally glancing up from his notes to see her teetering on the edge of her chair, as he lurched forward to catch her by the arm.

"Ms. Calloway!"

~DECEMBER 11, 2010~

Some light returns, but it is grey and undefined, a trail of shadow sliding in front of her face. There are still figures ... outlines really ... but she can no longer follow them, her eyes now drifting in circles, like a child chasing a butterfly's flight. Her mind swims and sinks. Her chest is weighted down. "GIVE HER ROOM!" someone shouts, and suddenly she realizes the reason for the interruption. For the commotion. Someone must be hurt. Someone must be in trouble. She strains her neck but can't see who. Too many dull grey shadows, hovering in the way. Why do they persist so? And so close. Why are they all jammed in so close? Why, they'll step on her gown! Her beautiful pale green gown.

"What are you doing?" she wants to call out, but she can make no sound. Where is my voice, she wonders, and instinctively instructs herself to calm down ... to focus and project ... *to the back wall and beyond, Miss Calloway.* Yes, Dr. Blaisdell. *If attention to detail cannot be achieved with the most rudimentary exercises, then it has no hope of being in attendance on the concert stage, Miss Calloway* ... Yes, yes, Dr. Blaisdell. But as she draws for air, she immediately grimaces, her only sound the groan of pain. Her chest is on fire. She can't breathe. Can't even begin to fill her lungs in the slightest.

"MY GOD, SOMEONE HELP HER!" The voice shouts again. She knows that voice. She's heard that voice before. "PLEASE, PLEASE ..." Its tone is so familiar, she feels like she can almost reach out and touch it, were it not for this grey cloud hovering ... this constant blur before her. Why is everything so goddamn grey? The ceiling, the faces. Her gown ... why has her beautiful, beautiful gown turned grey? "LOOK WHAT YOU'VE DONE, GODDAMN IT, ARE YOU HAPPY NOW?" The voice is right above her, crying out into the shadows as well. She can feel its breath. Feel it gasping and heaving in time with her own. Shallow, unsupported breath. "PLEASE, MOTHER ... PLEASE NO!" "I'm so sorry, Mother," she tries to call out, but the weight on her breast is suffocating. "I was so young and foolish." Her head flails from side to side, but she can see nothing. Her vision is but fog. Fog and rain. Yes, fog and rain … and she's running through it now. Running right through the midst of it.

"I couldn't do it, Mother. I couldn't do it … I'm sorry, Mother," she tries again, and then feels herself stumble. Down a steep hill. Steep and slippery. She loses her footing altogether and falls. A suitcase flies from her hand as she rolls over and over … all the way to the bottom of an old stone wall … beneath a doorway and a painted sign … She's unable to move. Face up, her flared nostrils and panting mouth catching the cold misty rain. And still … her chest is on fire.

Then out of the vision, out of the encroaching clouds, another voice calls her name. "MAGGIE! MAGGIE!" There is a faint hint of moonlight. Where has the concert gone, she wonders, and the voice calls again. "MAG-GIE!" She hears the footfall of someone running. Someone is looking for her. Someone is expecting her … expecting to find her here in this dreary grey abyss. Slowly she feels herself rising. She needs to go to this voice. Needs to find its source. And suddenly she too is running … racing through a frigid winter wind …stomping and crashing through hitherto unseen saplings and brittle leafless branches.

"MAGGIE!" She hears him again.

"Eli?"

She's distracted once more by the older panicky noises. "GIVE HER ROOM GODDAMN IT … GET A DOCTOR! FOR CHRIST'S SAKE, SOMEBODY GET A DOCTOR!" She is confused. She can't decide which voice is closer. She tries calling again. "ELI … ELI!" But the noise drowns out her attempts, filling up her tired ears and occupying the space above her head … the dull grey ill-defined space. She wants free of it, she decides. Wants free of the anger imploring her … HANG ON, MOTHER … *breathe, Miss Calloway* … HANG ON … *focus, Miss Calloway.* She wants

the cold wilderness instead. The cold and the wind rustling somewhere …
just beyond. She can hear it. Can almost feel it. But from where? Where is
she? Then comes the sound of panic once more … doors opening and closing. Sirens. Confusion. Fear. Echoing … then fading. Like a shadow passing
over the sun, she remembers … soaring by from grey to grey. Passing and
fading. Hanging on … then letting go …

~APRIL 1, 1982~

The detective yelled for help as soon as he saw her tumble forward. Almost immediately a stage hand and a couple of choir members were there,
helping Maggie back into her chair, fanning her, fetching and offering sips
of water. He, however, did not assist in the process. He was rather preoccupied instead by how the woman's spell, apart from startling him, had
actually proved quite informative. Clearly she had known this man. Clearly
there was a ⋯ a what? A fear? A loathing? Just from hearing his name?

Quietly he sent word through the stage manager, to inform the conductor, the chorus and orchestra that there would be a delay. Then he sent
some assistants to locate any of the building's architects and engineers,
even interior designers and decorators; anyone at all associated with the
building's construction who might be in attendance for the opening festivities. Soon, just like at the Distress Centre a few hours before, the detective found himself holding court, as he quickly went through the details of
his investigation, spelling out the trail that had brought him to Margaret
Calloway's dressing room, informing them all that a man named Eli Benowitz – a man police now know had been living on and off in street mis-
sions and psychiatric wards for a number of years – was the prime suspect
in the vandalism that had been found inflicted on their collective work

earlier that day. He explained that for months now this Eli Benowitz had been phoning help lines with plenty to say about the design, the construction and indeed the opening of Emerson Place. He told them that through some hasty investigating, his department was in possession of some personal effects that link this man not only to the concert hall, but to Margaret Calloway as well. Newspaper articles, album covers, pictures, all discovered not more than an hour ago in a shoebox – left in a locker at one of those shelters. The box, they learned upon examination, also contained bundles of unsent letters written to Ms. Calloway. Letters of a particularly negative and confrontational tone.

"This was probably the most recent," he stated, reaching into his overcoat and handing Maggie a folded piece of paper that appeared to have been, at some point, crumpled into a ball:

Maggie,

This is my last letter. Anything more would be pointless.

In the end I should have been your one true muse. Not some composer or conductor. Nor even your ignorantly adoring public. Me – the one who preceded that entire parade of adulation but was left to drown in the wake of all your pomp and success. Forgotten before I could fulfill MY calling. Fulfill what I yearned and dreamed to do. To create for you a perfect sanctuary for your voice. Create the very chamber where it might resonate for eternity. Inspire composers from beyond their graves, validate the conductors who rode the coattails of your success. Bring the masses to their knees.

That should have been us. Indeed could have been us, had you not strived so successfully to erase my very soul from the history of your life. And not just me but our child. Did you truly believe carrying the infant to term would redeem you? Carrying our child only to abandon him upon his very first breath? And yes … I know it was a son … Andrew. I have gone to great lengths

and travelled great distances – I have sacrificed the balance of
my life – to learn even just that one solitary fact. That one name.
Three years doing maintenance work at the hospital where you
gave birth to and then abandoned our son. Another year and
a half in construction, renovating the hall of records. All the
while biding my time. Waiting for my chance to slip away and
find the documents I needed to find. If only you had been this
courageous, Maggie. This resourceful. If only you had fought
harder for what was ours. If only you would have fought like
I have fought all these years. How different things could have
been. You, me … and Andrew makes 3.

But such was not your will. And you have left me no other
choice, but to finally answer a destiny of pain. Very soon there
will be a reckoning, Maggie. That is why this is my last letter.
That is why anything further would be pointless. Know that
when you step out onto Emerson's stage, Eli Benowitz will be
there … back in your perfect concert hall! And he will make you
pay forever.

"So would I be correct in assuming this man is not completely delusional, and that you did at some point have a relationship with him?" the
detective asked quietly, once he saw by her distant stare that Maggie had
finished reading the note. Vacantly she nodded, but was saved from further
scrutiny, at least momentarily, by one of the summoned foremen, looking
rather awkward in his tuxedo.

"Didn't we have a guy named Eli Berkowitz on site?"

"Benowitz," the detective corrected.

"Yeah, that's it." He turned to one of the other men now present. "Remember? The guy who hung around heckling the crew all the time? Jerry
finally hired him for occasional hours doing cleanup and odd jobs. Mostly
to get him out of our hair."

"Remember anything else about him?" Samuels asked, grabbing for a
pen once more.

"Just that it didn't work out. He was still more of a problem than a help. Jerry'd always find him off bothering the engineers. We had to let him go after a few days. Not before he laced into us something fierce though. Yelling and cursing how we were all a bunch of incompetent hacks. Accusing us of being too caught up making a sculpture out of the place to worry about the acoustics inside."

"That's the guy you're looking for?" one of the architects piped up. "Geez, he was something alright. I was there that day. I saw the whole show. But you know what? The funny thing is, despite all the F-bombs and the shouting, his arguments weren't completely off base."

"What are you on about?" another man spoke up.

"You were there too, John. You must have heard him. He had a lot to say about the design. About how the cavity within the structure had to be the essence of a concert hall. I mean, those were almost his exact words."

"Almost?" The detective raised an eyebrow.

"Well there was the profanity as well. Look all I'm saying is that despite all the swearing, and looking like death warmed over, the guy did seem to know a little something about acoustical design."

"With the emphasis on *little*," John, the other architect, countered.

"No, if you'll recall, he was quite specific in his criticisms. He said he questioned the interior walls. Whether their curvature was too gradual and needed more arc to ensure irregular reflections throughout the hall."

"And if he really knew what he was talking about, as you claim," John argued, "he'd know that we could never have accommodated a seating layout like that given our mandate, no matter how perfect the acoustics might be. It's simply not possible."

"And why is that?" the detective asked, jotting away with renewed vigour.

"Look, we were contracted to produce a 2,000-plus seat theatre. Given the parameters of the real estate in question, that presupposed certain limitations from the outset. The parcel of land here was shallow and wide, so to accommodate the desired capacity, we needed sizeable wings and a wide stage. The gradual curvature all but eliminates any parallel surfaces in the hall, which in turn eliminates the potential for null or reinforcing sound waves for the audience. So does the angled baffling, added behind the mezzanine. It is the optimal design for the space in question."

"But you have to admit, the guy understood that a circular design would take a sound source and ensure infinitely random sound reflections–"

"A circular design would be wonderful if you had the space. But a 2,056-seat circle downtown here? Hell, this isn't Stratford. You'd have to go up at least three tiers, maybe four. And I don't think all these well-heeled patrons and corporate donors would have been pleased with a building that looks like a four-storey beer can, would they?"

"A beer can?" the detective quizzed.

"A cylinder then," the architect clarified. "And yes I was there. And that's what your nut job was trying to tell us. That we should be building a cylinder."

"A cylinder?" Maggie joined in with a whisper, though the semicircle of strangers congregated next to her did not hear her, engrossed as they were in their own debate. She grabbed the letter once more, her eyes skimming over its cryptic testimony, the venom and the pain of his phrases working in concert to stab at her eyes – *Did you truly believe carrying the infant to term would redeem you? … I have sacrificed the balance of my life … It's pointless* – until she finally located the telling phrase …

… when you step out onto Emerson's stage, know that Eli Benowitz will be there … back in your perfect concert hall!

■

If at all, they would have seemed but a faint flash. A glimpse of light flickering, perhaps at the moment the violins began those soothing opening notes of her aria. Sent them soaring back through the chaos, back through the cold dark wilderness where he had been circling since the boundaries of time and space had first slipped away. If at all, it would have happened then (amidst the urgent yelps of a startled hound). Two shadows becoming one in an embrace of dappled moonlight on the forest floor, their words but wisps of breath … gentle wind against barren branches.

"Eli."

"You came."

"I'm so sorry…"

"Shhh …"

■

Margaret Calloway did not appear for the curtain call that opening night at Emerson Place, choosing instead to pin a note to the makeup mirror of her dressing room, that would inform the world of her immediate retirement from the concert stage.

Initially a *Toronto Star* review surmised that the announcement was performance-related, noting that the soprano's signature aria – her beloved *Redeemer Liveth* – was perhaps the flattest and the least inspiring version the diva had ever delivered. However, what that reviewer was not privy to – at least not at the time of filing her column – were the fateful backstage moments that had preceded the concert's third movement. She was not present to see the cold steel expression cross the great Margaret Calloway's face, nor see her stand amid the chaos of her dressing room and in a voice so completely void of the resonance for which she had been so long adored, hoarsely whisper, "You needn't worry, Gentlemen. If it's a bomb or arson you're worried about, I can assure you your precious building is safe tonight." Then, following a brief private discussion with a Metro Toronto detective – she strode from her dressing room to the wings of the stage to await the conclusion of her career.

By the time the revered diva stood to deliver one last aria, the call had been made … a squad car from the local OPP office dispatched … out along the old shore road and up the laneway to the old Calloway farm. Past the boarded-up farmhouse, not occupied since Maggie's parents had lived there decades earlier … past the cedar-railed yard, the old crumbling barn foundation … over to the structure to which they had been directed, stretching tall into the night sky. Inside, just as she had informed the detective they might, they found his body, lying in a heap at the foot of an old rotted ladder, up against the silo's tightly-curved stone wall.

~DECEMBER 12, 2010~

Christine Calloway-Avery lived in a large three-storey cut-stone house on the edge of the Conestoga River just outside the city limits of Waterloo. It was five in the morning by the time she steered her silver Audi (she never took the Smart Car into Toronto) up the gently curved driveway, lined with the recent addition of sandstone-coloured brick work – a detail that she had insisted the contractor redo, as the initial work had produced a far pinker hue than what was needed for a proper complement to the exterior of the home.

Hearing the sound of the car, her husband emerged from behind the frosted glass of the double-door main entrance and ran to meet her at the car door. Without prompting she launched in needlessly – for in truth they had been in continual contact since her mother's death – on the reasons for her being so long in coming. There was the matter of the death certificate at the hospital. Travel arrangements to be made for the funeral director. Calls left to the press, messages left for the lawyer's office. He allowed the litany to pass from her lips in a growing crescendo as she gathered her coat and belongings from the vehicle, until with one final slam of the door and one final, seething "This is all *her* fault" she marched up the walk and into her home, across the impenetrable sheen of her front vestibule's maple wood floor, up the plush white carpeting of the winding staircase (another detail that had proved deficient in its initial installation), down the second-floor hallway and through to the master bedroom. There she quickly changed from her now well-worn evening attire into the peach silk dressing gown that the maid had finally picked up from the dry cleaners the day before. She sat in front of her dressing mirror, applying liberal doses of cleansing cream to her face, and resumed the tirade that had begun back on the driveway. Allison would pay for her recklessness – playing Russian roulette with Mother's life like that! As soon as possible Christine would be speaking to her lawyers and taking appropriate action against that meddler responsible for her mother's demise. Likewise she would be discussing the suspect response time of the emergency services, their arrival having quite possibly been contributory to their failure to revive the woman. And then there was the theatre staff, so awkward and uncertain in their reaction. Yes, those responsible would pay, she vowed. "I'll make bloody sure," were her final words, the last thing from her lips before she finally looked up and glanced around at the expanse of her impeccably decorated boudoir – at the colonial-style dressing table before her, the large four-poster bed against the opposite wall, the west-facing sliding glass doors leading out to the second-storey terrace and the sunset view that for so long she had wanted to own. And there in that luxurious space that was the home of her dreams, with the sound of her husband's shoes just now padding against the pile of the staircase below, the daughter of the late Margaret Calloway broke down and wept.

~APRIL 2, 1982, SHORTLY PAST MIDNIGHT~

In a dimly-lit office located on the second floor of an unadvertised building which sat a certain number of blocks from Emerson Place, Henry Burgess thanked the detective for calling and explaining the outcome of the night's whirlwind investigation. He then hung up the phone, walked to the cabinet containing the files of the Centre's active callers and removed the folder marked 'Eli'. Closure of a sort, he told himself. Or at least the closest he ever got to such a concept in the never-ending cycle of calling-listening-calling-listening.

In the morning he would ask Irene to move the file downstairs to storage, also to return the volunteer file which he had pulled from the bowels of the building earlier that night. For now, though, he felt tired and it was time to go home. Instinctively he slapped his pants pocket to check on the whereabouts of his wallet and keys, then pushed his roll-chair towards the coat tree that held his windbreaker, stubbing the front wheels on the same turned-up corner of the rug. Maybe tomorrow he would look into a replacement as well, he thought, reaching for the light switch on the wall.

"I prefer a little more light in there, if you don't mind," came the quiet voice from through the doorway in the room behind him.

"Oh Andrew, I'm sorry," the facilitator apologized, scrambling back through the darkened room – stubbing the rug again – to paw for the chain on his desk lamp. "How's that?" he called over his shoulder.

"Better, thanks," the young man replied, getting up to join the facilitator in his office. "Um, I'm just between calls so I kind of overheard. Eli killed himself?"

"That's how it seems," Henry nodded. "Turns out he wasn't in the city at all. They found him on a farm a few hours north of here ... up by Georgian Bay. Apparently he jumped from a ladder inside an old corn silo."

"Wow," the volunteer mouthed, and slowly lowered himself down to perch on the edge of the sofa.

"You OK, Andrew?" The volunteer nodded absently, staring out the darkened window. Like he was looking for something that was no longer there, Henry surmised. "Funny how he was really never angry when you talked to him," he noted.

Andrew nodded, his thoughts and glance both still elsewhere.

"But definitely depressed, yes?"

"Oh way beyond depressed," Andrew returned. "You know, he actually spent a lot of time apologizing. 'I'm intruding,' he'd say. 'It's not fair for me to be intruding.' I'd tell him it wasn't an intrusion in the least ... that I was there to listen. But like I mentioned, that only seemed to make him all the sadder. Did the police tell you anything more about him? Or can you say?"

Henry shrugged. "He was in and out of some institutions and shelters. Sometimes just homeless on the street. But it sounds like he was a pretty intelligent person. Certainly educated. And he certainly wasn't always so down and out. I don't know if he ever mentioned it to you, but he lived and worked in England for quite a long time. And by the way, judging by that trace of an accent I hear, am I correct in thinking that's where you once called home?"

Andrew nodded. "Maybe he took to my voice because it reminded him of somebody over there."

"Maybe. Anyway, turns out he worked on the construction sites for three or four big renovation projects in and around London. His medical files list them very specifically. Very intentionally, you'd even say. Like he wanted someone to know. Like part of his plan was to leave some sort of trail. At least that's what Detective Samuels figures. And I have the feeling there's something to it. I mean, even tonight, once they got the lead about the farm up north, they canvassed the bus station. Right away they managed to find people there who said they definitely saw him. The woman at the wicket remembered a guy plopping down his exact fare in rolled quarters. Told the police how proud he seemed that he had enough money for the bus ticket and a cab ride at the other end, he told her. But it's really all a bit strange yet, isn't it? After all, killing himself really didn't need all this planning did it? I mean, there's plenty of traffic close by to just step in front of."

"Unless he wasn't."

"What do you mean?"

"Planning to … you know. Couldn't falling off a ladder be as plausible as jumping off one?"

"I suppose. Either way, I don't know what the attraction of an old farm silo would have been. Pretty cold and empty way to go, if you ask me."

And suddenly, with his reply, the facilitator realized he had been completely wrong. There was no closure to this after all. No closure whatsoever. "Guess we'll never know," he sighed, once again checking for his keys.

"Reckon not," the young man agreed.

"There was one interesting thing I did learn, though. It turns out he actually volunteered here for a few months back in '74. Who knows? Maybe you two worked some shifts or two."

Andrew shrugged. "I couldn't really say. I've been at this eight years. I've seen so many people come and go."

"Well, he wouldn't have gone by Eli. Apparently he used the name *Andrew 03* on the phone lines."

"The same name he'd call and ask for?"

Henry nodded. "I don't suppose you can remember anyone–"

But the young man was shrugging and shaking his head before Henry could finish the question. Then came the shrill ring of the phone from the other room.

"Well … duty calls."

"Yup. Go ahead," Henry replied and got as far as the doorway before he turned back into the Centre and tiptoed back to Andrew's position at the call desk. "Sorry to interrupt, but I just wanted to apologize for calling you in on that meeting earlier. Must have seemed like a bit of an ambush."

"No, don't worry about it. Glad to help," he answered in a whisper, his hand blocked over the receiver.

"But on the same night as you're staying in for the overnight ... I should have checked the roster first."

"Really no trouble at all ... oh ... yes, sorry, Caller ... no, just some office confusion here. I apologize. No ... I'm listening now. On we go ..."

Henry said good night with a silent wave and a nod, then finally turned toward the door for good. Yes, he nodded in agreement as he reached the hallway. In the absence of closure ... on we go.

The Amens

Peter glanced over at Kyle. The finish line was approaching and everyone in the concert hall was unified in its rich fulfillment of music and text. Fitting, he mused. After all, in the final analysis, it is the audience that completes such a performance. And not merely by word or applause or critique. Of course, those enterprises are inevitable upon the concert's conclusion, but they are after the fact. No, the final act, the young man concluded with a silent gulp of anticipation, lies indeed within the concert proper, and it consists of nothing more than taking in the music. Taking it in to its very last decay of sound ... and receiving it.

> *To receive power and riches and wisdom and*
> *strength and honour and glory and blessing*

His heart was full, for the joy of this masterpiece – the joy that had never failed to leave him swimming in his own silent tears – was now multiplied. He loved Kyle. Loved that he was listening and opening himself up to explore someone else's passion. Loved that he, so retiring and careful in his life now sat straight and attentive, shoulders forward, away from the seat back, his own tears clearly forming in the very corner of his eye just as they had for Peter so many years ago. Loved that this shy and careful man now sought out Peter's hand and gathered it into his own as he watched, listened and took in this wonderful spectacle in all its glory.

"Someday," he suddenly heard the old man in the street echoing in his head, just as the crescendo of the choir turned onto the last page of their final chorus ... the entire score from top to bottom, the clear soaring trumpet lines joining forces with the churn of voices, the strident strings, the low ground of the pipe organ's pedals, the pulsing heartbeat of the pounding tympani – streaming together into one unbelievable highway of sound, united in their charge to the brink of its climax, before stopping suddenly and teetering on the edge of conclusion ... the unfinished dominant chord, the final words ... Forever, and ever ... leaving the audience's collective ears in need of more ...

Then began the slow ascent of the Amens, starting with bass strings and voices before urgently gathering others to their midst as they cycled through choir and orchestra, building and building ...

Peter looked over again. This was it. The stirring culmination that never failed to take him somewhere else, to transport him to realms he could not hope to find on his own. One last brief respite, courtesy of the violin section, and then the wall of sound hit, the melody crashing over Emerson Place with strings and percussion, with trumpet and organ pipe ... and with the entire choir led by the first sopranos with their high A entry. Then Handel's final surprise – the treasure of the flattened 7th descending to that penultimate phrase ... and then the pause ... one last breath before the final Amen would be proclaimed ... proclaimed with every available sound.

Peter breathed into the pause. "Someday," he whispered, and squeezed his loved one's hand.

■

To Mr. Drew Stafford
c/o Cherry Blossom Records

September 5, 1987

Dear Mr. Stafford,

My name is Murray Page and I'm a retired arena manager in a small town up here in Ontario, Canada. I am also a big fan of your song Broken Angels. My wife and I first heard The River City Shufflers singing it on our local radio station shortly before she died a couple of years back. You see, my wife had been quite ill that last year and she was pretty much confined to her bed, so listening to music was one of the last joys she had. We'd often sit together in the evenings, her in bed and me in a recliner that I had moved into the bedroom.

It's a great little song, Mr. Stafford. You should be proud of it. In fact, when Helen passed away I asked a local band to play it for her funeral and they did a splendid job. Why, even my granddaughter's music teacher thinks it's good and she used to be a famous opera type of a singer, travelling all over the world. In fact, she once told me the notes at the start of Broken Angels remind her a lot of a solo she used to sing. So that's pretty high praise.

You see, my granddaughter came to live with me a few months
after my wife died. Her mom also passed away and her dad took
off. I don't want to go into it too much, just to say that she was
one sad and troubled girl for quite some time. And it wasn't till
I had her signed up for those singing lessons that she started
showing some life again. Which I guess is my point for writing.
Because what those lessons did for my Ally is more or less what
your Broken Angels song did for me. And I just wanted to write
and say thanks.

Sincerely,
Murray Page

~DECEMBER 12, 2010~

He met her at their house. It was the least he could do after the frantic
phone call that had awakened him from his dozing in front of the small
TV he kept in his room. It was the only thing, given the thought of Allison
driving home all alone, upset as she would undoubtedly be. He was dozing
again in the cab of his pickup when her car finally came creeping around
the corner and into the driveway. He turned the key long enough to illumi-
nate the dash board clock – 4:30 a.m. – then sprang from the truck to let
her fall into his arms. Almost lifeless herself, he thought.

"She just collapsed, Grandpa. Just went over in the middle of the concert. By the time the ambulance was there and they had her out in the lobby
… they tried to bring her back but … What have I done? Oh God, what
have I done?"

He grabbed onto her and instantly a flood of memories came crashing
over him … holding and squeezing the 11-year-old girl who had shrieked
herself awake as she fled from the terror of some nightmare borne – he was

certain – not of any dream world, but from the hell that life had handed her. He recalled how he would have to hang on so. No cradling nor rocking, just a two-handed immobilizing grasp that no matter how seemingly smothering was still never enough for her. "Tighter Grandpa ... Tighter ... don't let go, OK? Don't ever?" It was the memory of the last time she had truly needed him. The last time he had undeniably understood his role.

"You made good time," he mumbled haplessly.

"Christine wanted me out of there," she stammered into the lapel of his coat. "And she's right. As impossible as she's been over the years, she's absolutely right. This is all my fault. What in God's name was I thinking? Her age, and as weak as she was ...what the hell was I thinking?" The words grew fainter as her hands formed fists around bunched-up handfuls of her grandfather's parka and, without realizing what she was doing, she began pushing and pounding at his chest. "This is all my fault ... I did this!"

"Now stop that, Ally. Stop that sort of talk right there."

"And now I've made you get up out of bed ... my God, how long have you been waiting here?"

"Allison, I said that's enough." Gently he shook her by the shoulders until her eyes – the same eyes of her childhood – finally rolled up to meet his. "There now. That's better," he said. "Now, first off ... I'm here because you and me, we look out for each other, don't we? ... Don't we?" Allison nodded weakly. "So where else would I want to be at a time like this? Second, I'm here because you shouldn't be in this old house all by yourself. God knows the place has seen more than enough of somebody holed up inside ... grieving all alone ..."

This time it was his voice that faltered and only then did Allison realize that not all of the sniffling and sobbing that had been filtering through the damp night air had been coming from her. "I tried, Ally. I did. But all that running around, doing double shifts at the arena, and passing you off from sitter to sitter ... that was no way for a young girl to–"

"Grandpa, no. It wasn't like that."

"It was. Goddamn that car crash that took your mother away. God-damn the disease that took Helen, too. She woulda done a lot better by you, ya know ... a lot better."

She reached out to grab onto his coat once more, this time to console the shaking figure within, and in so doing felt a wisp of air in her lungs, air that had been missing ever since she had turned to see her mentor fallen on the beautiful royal blue broadloom of Emerson Place earlier that evening. "Grandpa, please don't think this way."

"So I'm here because ... because you just shouldn't have to walk into that house all by yourself. Not tonight, anyway. All full of guilt and down on yourself, like I figured you'd be." His eyes avoided her, fixed instead on the line of snow he shuffled between his boots. "'Cause no matter how bad you are right now ... no matter how responsible that daughter of hers is trying to make you feel ... you gotta know that it's just her own grief looking for somewhere to scream. My God, Ally, after all the things you've done for that lady? The time you made for her? You were the friend. Not her daughter. And you gotta know ... there's nobody prouder of anybody ... than I am of–"

Again his words ebbed, giving way in their absence to the sound of uncertain feet working back and forth till he could only weakly whisper, "OK?"

Allison took her grandpa's face in her hands and leaned her forehead to his.

"Grandpa?" she asked. "Can we go for a drive?"

■

The road out to the Calloway house had changed over the years. The bends and curves, once just a ribbon of gravel along vacant shoreline, were now lined with nothing but the town's proudest money – as Mur-ray Page was wont to say. Waterfront estates with lavish gardens and opu-lent mansions of cut stone and fresh ivy, old in design but new in age – a facade of history stretching tall to block off the once egalitarian view of the shoreline.

He had begun his tirades about these changes even back in her childhood, on the many trips out for lessons, when these relentless rows of grandeur had yet been only a handful of ambitious building projects. And Allison had always nodded in compliant, albeit absent-minded agreement, her eyes inevitably peering instead toward the older modest dwellings on the opposite side of the road. They were always her preference. Perhaps because they looked more lived-in. Happier. She had two favourites: a powder blue board-and-batten cottage and a rich green farmhouse with white trim. Both sat in fairly close proximity to one another, five miles or so past the outskirts of town, at the point where the escarpment bluffs broke free from the tree-covered ridge into a dramatic rocky cliff face that loomed as backdrop for these little houses and the pastures that lay about them. Driving by had always made her feel as if she were filming the opening panorama of some movie – the story of house and home perhaps – with that steadfastly immovable outcropping juxtaposed behind the motion of rolling past those little homesteads. As if she were capturing the movement of life by simply leaning her head against the truck window and letting the scene wash past. It had been especially effective in the low late-day sun. Now, however – without even the faintest promise of daylight …

"I didn't even get to say good-bye," she whispered and closed her eyes.

■

He parked halfway up the laneway, manoeuvring in such a way that the windshield took in the farmhouse, the yard and the old barn foundation all in one.

She leaned against his arm. "Did you get to say goodbye to Grandma?" she asked. Murray nodded, shifting his weight to wrap his hand around her shoulder. "Well," he drawled, "I won't lie. Getting your timing right to say a goodbye like that is tough. 'Cause you don't want to make it that final. You want to hang on. But here's the thing, Ally. Not to speak ill or anything, but as far as saying goodbye or saying thanks is concerned, I think she's the one who missed out. I mean, when you were getting all upset there back at the house, wondering what you were thinking driving her all the way down there … well, it seems to me you were taking her to the one place she truly belonged. And if you ask me, I think the fact she died in the middle of that concert was a blessing."

Allison raised her head.

"I know. I may be way off base, but all I'm saying is that maybe going in the middle of something you loved to do is the best way to go. Damn sight better than finishing off everything you could think to do or say in life and then just sitting around waiting for the end. Like that composer … the one you told me about who never got done his orchestra what-ya-call-it?"

His granddaughter rolled her eyes. "Symphony, Grandpa. It's called the *Unfinished Symphony* and it's by Schubert."

"Well like I said, and I may be just rambling away here, but it seems to me that despite all the upset people there probably were when he passed away, if good ole Schubert went with his composing pen firm in his hand, well he probably died a happy man."

She considered this for a moment, then straightened up, reached for the door and got out of the truck to examine the farmhouse a little more closely.

Murray watched her go, her hands in her pockets, head up, seemingly trying to take in every detail of this building that had served as such a refuge; such a *home*. Then he watched as she heaved a lengthy sigh and, with the sag of overwhelming emotion, sank to her knees. Quickly he got out and went to her.

"I'm such a fool," she declared in the midst of her tears. "We're all such fools." Murray started to interject something, something to allay what sounded to his ears like another wave of guilt gathering to break over her, but then he noticed – thanks to the beam of the headlights – that although she was slumped forward on the ground and shaking her head, the hint of a smile had actually begun to creep across her face. "All our etiquette and decorum. All our seriousness for the things that we love. You know?"

Her grandfather's expression informed her that indeed he did not.

"You've been right all along, Grandpa," she continued nonetheless. "I have been living my life through Maggie. I have invested so much energy in her life and her past–"

"Ah let's not talk bout that now, Ally. I was wrong to stick my nose–"

"No. That's just it. You weren't! Not at all. I mean, after all those lessons and recitals, was this really the best outcome? A life of vicarious pleasure sitting over tea and crumpets week in and week out, waiting for Maggie to reveal some little tidbit about her exciting singing career? Because at this point, that's my legacy. And why? Because at the root of it all, I'm still this scared little kid, naïve enough to believe that all those lessons were their own goal – the gold star and the good-little-girl pat on the head. I never understood ... never appreciated what they really were for someone like Maggie Calloway. The scales and the exercises ... all of it. Tools. Nothing more. Tools for the creation of passion ... like a sculptor moving his hands against clay ... or a painter with his brush and canvas ... or like ..." She hesitated a moment, then Murray noticed her grin spread wider ... "like a lover's skilled touch–"

"Oh Allison, I'm your grandfather, for crying out loud."

"Well then you had best cover up those modest grandfather ears of yours, because I'm afraid what I have to say isn't the stuff of good little granddaughters going to their singing lessons. Not if I'm going to say goodbye properly. Not if I'm going to thank her properly. And not just for the lessons and the Saturday afternoons ... but for the passion, Grandpa."

Murray's eyes dropped to his boot tops.

"And not just from me. No, this is on behalf of every shy, retiring patron of the concert hall who ever flocked to hear one of her concerts. To
hear proficiency transform into rapture. I mean true rapture ... and we,
in spite of our inhibitions, came away transcended, for once not merely
lauding the technical skills of a piece well sung with our polite little nods
and our tippy-tap applause. No we came away transported, thanks to the
effortlessness of those techniques, all those regimented vocal exercises that
we ourselves could never see past. Could never make out of our clay with
our feeble little tools. We who could never dare stray past the propriety
of gold stars and pats on the head, past the safety of teaching the school
choirs, past the polite little compartment made for the discipline of music
by the unaffected world at large. Where art is reduced to mere curriculum.
Like a times table or a spelling quiz. That's the sum of us, the gold-star
girls – the casualties of Kiwanis festivals from here to God knows where.
So when we finally find ourselves in the presence of greatness we swallow
up as much as we can. Because all too soon we will be back inside our own
skin, hurrying home to ... to what? Pack the kids' lunches for school the
next morning? Press a shirt for hubby's work?"

"Check up on old granddad in the home?" Murray mumbled, his eyes
still aimed at the ground.

"But at least for those brief moments, her voice made love to us."

"Ah Ally. Geez–"

"Yes, Grandpa. Like the perfect caresses we always imagined from that
perfect lover, in our dreams, the Maggie Calloways of this world let us slip
away into our other skins ... our passionate skins ... and experience a few
seconds of bliss ... and abandon ... and ..."

Murray finally dared glance up, a decided wince firmly in place, until
he noticed that – for the moment anyway – the tears had subsided. Her
gaze was now flung toward the rolling fields and the distant bay slowly
coming into focus with the first hint of dawn.

"…and the beauty," she finished with a smile. "The beauty we don't have the wherewithal to find ourselves."

The moment was interrupted by a series of high-pitched barks echoing from the line of trees up against the cliffs behind them, a distraction for which Murray Page – if he were honest – was not entirely ungrateful.

"That old Polly?" he asked, turning to peer up towards the rock.

Allison nodded. "Probably. The nurse was supposed to let her back in yesterday morning after we left," she sighed, sending a puff of breath into the cold morning air. "I'll have to make some arrangements for her, I suppose. She can't stay here now."

■

Soon they climbed back in the truck and headed for town.

"Grandpa?" she asked, instinctively leaning her head back against the window.

"Mmm?"

"I'm thinking of adding on to the house. Putting in a music room off the back. Opening the place up a little brighter."

"Mmm."

"And I'm thinking of getting back in touch with the regional choir. Maybe auditioning for their summer season. What do you think of that?"

Murray Page squinted into the emerging dawn as he steered out the lane and down the shore road back toward town. For once, without a single mitigating word of deference, he delivered perhaps as definitive a reply as the man had ever offered in his lifetime.